ELEPHANT GUN MALONE

A Sioux war party sent a year of Matt Malone's hard work down the pan. But when he joined a wagon train as a scout on its trail to Oregon and met lovely widow Mary Franklin, Matt believed that his troubles were over. However, even on his wedding day the shadow of death still bit at his heels in the shape of the vengeful Smith brothers and the Snake River Shoshoni Indians. Would he ever be free?

Books by Ed Hunter
in the Linford Western Library:

BULLION MASSACRE
DOUBLE D SHOWDOWN

ED HUNTER

ELEPHANT GUN MALONE

Complete and Unabridged

LINFORD
Leicester

First published in Great Britain in 1994 by
Robert Hale Limited
London

First Linford Edition
published 1996
by arrangement with
Robert Hale Limited
London

The right of Ed Hunter to be identified as
the author of this work has been asserted
by him in accordance with the
Copyright, Designs and Patents Act, 1988

British Library CIP Data

Hunter, Ed
Elephant gun Malone.—Large print ed.—
Linford western library
1. English fiction—20th century
I. Title
823.9′14 [F]

ISBN 0–7089–7916–5

Published by
F. A. Thorpe (Publishing) Ltd.
Anstey, Leicestershire

Set by Words & Graphics Ltd.
Anstey, Leicestershire
Printed and bound in Great Britain by
T. J. Press (Padstow) Ltd., Padstow, Cornwall

This book is printed on acid-free paper

1

MATT MALONE turned to see the Sioux braves still dogging his trail, and drawing closer. He lashed his tiring horse with the ends of the reins. The going had become much harder since they had left the flat ground behind. Now they climbed in a jerky scramble up a steep scree-covered slope to seek the protection of the trees on the plateau above. If he could make it to there, then there was a chance for him to keep his hair.

The lead-rope tightened between his horse and the mule. The horse slowed, so he kicked hard with his heels to spur the animal on.

"God damn it, Delila." He cursed the huge black delta-type mule trailing reluctantly behind. "Are you aimin' to get my scalp lifted?" He felt the saddle horn of the riding horse, and tightened under his leg again like a bar of iron as the cantankerous Delila resisted. "Move yer lazy arse, before I skin the hide off it."

Matt constantly kicked, sweated and swore as the reluctant pack-animal dragged its heels every inch of the way like a reluctant bride. They eventually made it to the edge of the trees. Twisting in his saddle he turned to check on the redskins. Then he reined in to take a more prolonged, sweeping look. To his surprise there was no sign of his pursuers.

"Well I'll be a monkey's uncle," he muttered. "Where in the hell've they got to?"

If the Sioux braves had really called it off, he wasn't going to complain. It had taken a year's hard work, trapping, skinning and drying out the prime pelts loaded on to the pannier frames across the mule's back. Matt had plans for the money they'd bring when he reached the trading post at Fort Laramie.

After another five miles, still without sight or sound of the Indians, the cooling shade offered by the overhead branches was pleasant. He began to relax. Maybe he had been wrong all along and need not have worried. Perhaps it had just been a hunting party he had seen, travelling in his direction. Perhaps! He still wasn't all that certain.

The trees began to thin out and soon he found himself riding into bright sunshine again. Heading south-east once more, the trail led him through a natural corridor of granite boulders, scattered and left there by some prehistoric glacier. Now, instead of cold, the boulders reflected the sun's heat like an enormous oven, and he began to consider taking time out for a rest.

The eyeball-scorching brightness caused him to close his eyes, content to let his horse find its own path between the rocks. In this fashion he rode on for a time, ignoring the flies which buzzed around in swarms, tormenting man and beast alike. Letting the sweat trickle from his face and drip off his chin as it pleased, he sagged in his saddle and cooked.

A mile and a half further on his horse slowed, then came to a halt.

Almost asleep, Matt cracked open his eyes, then shot bolt upright. Now wide awake, every nerve tingled and his heart raced fast enough to burst.

"How in hell did they get there?"

Straddled across his path, a semi-circle of stone-faced Sioux bucks sat their ponies. Each brave was painted ready for war and dyed eagle feathers fluttered from their shining black, bear-greased braids.

One, holding himself more aloof than the rest, stood out as the leader. Crammed on his head he proudly wore a white woman's ludicrous straw bonnet, bedecked in artificial fruits and multi-coloured feathers. But what turned Matt Malone's stomach was the sight of the leader's coup stick. From it dangled six scalps, one long and curly blonde, and the others ginger, of varying sizes, all no doubt taken from the same family.

Malone noticed only two of the bucks carried firearms, ancient muzzle loaders, at best only fit for shooting at sitting bush turkeys, at worst, a deadly danger to those who risked firing them at all. From behind the small, round buffalo-hide shields which the braves carried, the protruding heads of decorated war axes advertised that this was no hunting party.

On the left of the line, a couple of the Indians, a mite keener than the others, had their bows ready drawn, on aim, with each barbed arrow pointed directly at him.

Feeling sick in his stomach but clinging on to hope, Matt forced his lips into a smile which split his shocked face. Holding up his open hand, palm forward in front of him for all to see, he gave the universal sign of peace.

"Hi, fellas," he said. "Er . . . how!

Er . . . any of you guys speak English, eh?"

None of the braves smiled. Instead they twisted their eyebrows and furrowed the skin on their brows as they considered the unfamiliar words.

Matt's tongue attempted to wet his lips, but failed. He tried to swallow but could not. His mind scraped the bottom of his mental barrel seeking ideas and before speaking again he had to cough to clear his throat. When the words came again, the huskiness of his voice betrayed his anxiety.

"*Parlez vous Français?*" he tried in desperation, in spite of the fact that these were the only words of French that he knew. But that was no problem for there was no response to that either. He jabbed his finger at his chest, all the time trying to sustain the smile. "Friend . . . me good friend."

Twang! Something whistled close by his head and he knew without any doubt that there would be no pow-wow that day. He ducked low. His gun-hand slapped leather at speed and brought up his Colt to align the barrel with the nearest brave. The hammer thumbed back two clicks as his crooked forefinger already applied pressure to the trigger.

The daubed white and ochre warpaint on the face of his first target was splattered with blood, and before the buck careered backwards over the rear of his pony, Matt snapped off more shots. Instinctively, not using the sights, he blasted two more, dug in his spurs and rode directly at the line-up.

His aggressive tactic worked. Eager to avoid his charging animals and rapid firing, the braves were for the moment unable to use their weapons.

The shoulder of Matt's steed collided with a rearing palomino pony, sending it and its rider careering sideways into another Indian's mount. Both ponies and their riders crashed to the ground, creating pandemonium among the frantically dancing hooves of the others about them.

"Come on Delila," Matt yelled, but he need not have bothered. For once that day, his mule needed no coaxing or swearing to get her to move. Like a greyhound slipped free to chase game, she surged forward, through the screaming Sioux, her long ears pressed back, following as fast as she could go.

Above her sideways-swaying load, more bullets from Matt's pistol zipped through the air. Long before their final journey had been planned, two more bucks had been dispatched to the happy hunting grounds.

From somewhere behind, Matt was conscious of someone else firing a single shot. Almost at the same moment, the lead rope went bar-tight and his horse jerked to a sudden stop. Its hindquarters skidded, half turning to the left, and almost going down on its haunches, came close to unseating him before struggling back to its feet again.

The nightmare happened within the

8

space of a few seconds. Beside him, Delila lay kicking, her mouth open and tongue lolling out helplessly. Blood gushed out on to the ground, pumped from a gaping musketball wound in the side of her neck.

"Jesus," Matt swore as the fingers of his left hand fumbled frantically to cast the looped end of the headrope free from the saddle horn. Then, he leaned down, his arm outstretched to shorten the range, his pistol firing a single shot in Delila's brain.

Even as the mule kicked her last, Malone had already urged his now unrestrained horse, into a breakneck gallop, dodging the flying arrows as he weaved in and out between the rocks.

When the arrows had stopped flying, Matt turned his head to see why. All but three of the braves who still lived were gathered around Delila's corpse, looting her load. But the other three, intent upon glory, came on after him, each of them keen to be the one to slaughter him, and add a prized white-man's scalp to his collection.

"Murderin' robbin' bastards," he cursed to his sweating horse, unable to permit his blue roan gelding to slacken speed. "All that time an' work and for what?" The horse twitched its ears as though waiting for the answer. "They've got everythin' I had . . . and the damned heathens are still comin' after me!"

Using only knee pressure to control his tiring mount, Malone ejected the empty shell cases from the cylinder of his pistol, reloading with spares from the storage loops of his gunbelt. Just in time, he snapped the final bullet into place as the leading Sioux rider drew alongside and leaned in closer, his tomahawk raised for the kill.

Matt swerved his horse to the left causing the brave to miss his chance by inches. The Indian, a born chancer, came in for a second try, but was too late. The freshly loaded revolver spat lead into his ribs from point-blank range. With a look of disbelief on his face, the dead buck slipped from the pony's back and bounced awkwardly along the ground like a flopping side of bacon.

"And now it's your turn fella," Malone muttered through clenched teeth as the next Indian closed in to do battle.

It did not happen that way. One moment Matt was squeezing the trigger, and the next he was flying through the air, then bouncing along the trail. Sky and land spun wildly and the air was being driven from his body with each bone-shaking bounce. As in a dream he saw his horse tumbling along beside him. He tasted dry trail dust and felt it grit between his teeth.

After what seemed a million years, the earth stopped trying to beat him to death and stopped its crazy spinning. Lying on his back, gulping in great rib-heaving gasps of air, Malone gazed up at the sky. He was aware of hoof-beats coming to a halt nearby, then a high pitched screech, like that of a stooping hawk, sounded as a shadow blacked out the sky again.

Already screaming his hate, the eager young Sioux landed, straddling Matt, knocking the wind from his lungs again. One hand of the brave clutched Matt's hair, forcing his head to the ground, while his other hand held the raised tomahawk, fighting against Malone's desperate two-handed grasp.

Malone suddenly heaved sideways, and together the adversaries rolled over and over, the axe trapped between them. Then the axe was free and swinging. Matt jerked his head to his right, only just avoiding the blade, but the hickory haft struck him a glancing blow which removed skin from his cheek. Lashing out with his fist he had the satisfaction of feeling the crunch as the Sioux's nose flattened beneath his bunched knuckles. Then both rolled in different directions, scrambled cat-like to their feet and stood hunched, ready to resume the battle.

Each circled cautiously, watching

every move. The Sioux waved his axe from side to side like a snake about to strike. Matt felt for his gun but the holster was empty. Then he remembered it being knocked from his grasp when his gelding had gone down.

The redskin smirked and drew the extended fingers of his free hand across his own throat to show his intentions. He began to close in, his moccasined feet making no sound. Advancing, he made tentative swings with the axe, forcing his quarry back towards the big rocks.

Weaponless, Matt backed steadily, keeping just out of range of the swinging blade, but the confident brave came on relentlessly. Then it happened. One moment Matt was up on his feet, the next, he had caught the heel of his boot against a couple of small rocks and was flat on his back again. The Indian rushed in, whooping and swinging up his tomahawk to end it all.

Malone felt the rock under his

hand. It was little bigger than his own clenched fist but he grabbed it and thanked the Lord. Just as the war axe was about to descend and split his skull, Matt hurled the stone.

The Sioux brave dropped to his knees then fell forward, his bloody face pulped and unrecognizable. At his side the war axe clattered harmlessly on to the brothers of the rock which had killed him.

The third brave, the one Malone had forgotten about, materialized out of nowhere and, yelling war cries, rode his painted pony directly at him.

Crouching now, his knees bent and tensioned like springs, Matt awaited the next attack. The charging pony's unshod hooves scattered the stones in all directions as its whooping rider aimed his lance. With only a foot to spare, Malone flung himself clear of the levelled lance, but stumbled and fell over the man he had just killed. As the latest adversary wheeled for a second charge, Matt snatched up the

14

fallen tomahawk.

"Right, ya red varmint," he growled. "Just you try that move again." With a weapon in his hand he stood a chance, but he was not crazy. It would be too easy to let the redskin trap him against the big rocks, so he darted out, into the open again.

This time he held his ground with more confidence. Dodging aside, he grabbed the end of the lance. His free hand caught and gripped the shaft just behind the point. Digging in his heels and leaning back, he heaved. The warrior held on. Matt held on. And the pony galloped on.

A dull thud sounded and a cloud of trail dust stirred up as the floundering brave crashed to earth. Before he could recover, Malone leapt into action and with one swift blow, buried the blade of the axe, nose deep, through the top of the redskin's skull.

"Well . . . that's another good Indian," Matt mumbled, wiping his blood and brain-spattered hands on the buckskin leggings of the cadaver. He looked around in case there should be other attackers waiting. But there were none. A movement close by caused his nerves to twang with tension. His horse, still down on its side, lifted its great head as it struggled vainly to get to its feet.

"Whoa there, old pal," Malone cautioned kindly. "Let's see what yer trouble is." Calmly moving towards the stricken animal, he pursed his lips and shook his head. "I guess this is where you an' me take separate trails. You hang in there; I'll not be more'n a minute."

Backtracking, he found his revolver. It was useless. One of the ponies must have stepped on it, pushing the cylinder out, bending both the mechanism and the barrel.

"G'damned Indians," he snarled. With a petulant display of venom he hurled the ruined gun as far as his strength would allow. "Now things've got t' be done the hard way."

Feeling in his pants pocket he

brought out the pocket knife he always carried. His thumb scraped against the biggest blade. It felt sharp, but not sharp enough for what he had to do. Crouching down beside the gelding's head he picked up a small flat piece of rock. Spitting on it, he talked soothingly to the animal as he carefully wet the blade.

When his thumb told him that the blade was as sharp as it ever was going to be, he moved closer and patted the animal's arched neck.

"It's all right, fella. This ain't gonna hurt too much . . . I promise." The fingers of his left hand felt for and found a suitable vein close to the surface of the skin. "Steady, boy."

He held the freshly honed blade still for a second remembering times past, then slipped the steel silently through the skin to sever the chosen blood vessel. To Matt's relief the horse never even flinched.

The blade having done its work, he wiped it clean then returned it to his pocket. After that he waited, fondly patting the powerful neck again and stroking the white starred forehead.

"Told ya it wouldn't hurt none."

Malone stayed with his horse all the time as its life-blood drained from the cut he had made. Like a good friend he comforted it with his hands and soothed it with words until old man death finally claimed the animal for his own.

"S'long, partner." He stood and looked at the redskin cadavers. They were already covered in flies. Shifting his gaze skywards, he saw buzzards circling eagerly, black silhouettes of death, waiting for him to go.

A thought provoked him to scan the area for the dead Indians' ponies, but he was disappointed. The scrawny animals had all high-tailed it, probably back the way they had come. Wistfully he eyed the hazy-blue chain of distant mountains. He sighed heavily, and with an expressive shrug, bent to retrieve his saddle, bridle and bedroll.

"Seems like I've got me a hell of a walk."

★ ★ ★

The other Indians were unlikely to come after him in the dark. Also, it was much cooler to march through the night.

By the time daybreak arrived, the mountains had begun to look real. The trail grew tougher the nearer he got to the pass. Inside his narrow-toed, high-heeled boots, his feet felt like they were on fire, and the skin on both of his shoulders had been rubbed raw by their unusual load.

Apart from the briefest of rests, Malone kept right on going, every step taking him closer to where he aimed for. He planned to stop and make camp at noon, eat, then find some shade where he could sleep until the sun had gone and his march would recommence.

Sweating, footsore and weary, he

topped another scrub-covered ridge shortly before midday. He blinked into the heat haze, then grinned as wide as an open gate.

"Matt Malone," he whispered to himself, "this is your lucky day."

2

MATT MALONE wearily worked his way down towards the closely grouped conestogas on the other side of the creek, wondering why they were there at all. Oxen and draught horses, still in good condition, grazed peacefully along the bank, slightly downstream. Something was not right. Normally such a wagon train would be on the move at this time of day.

The smell of woodsmoke and snatches of voices carried on the slight breeze, came to him across the slow-running water, but as yet he saw no one.

Too tired to bother searching for stepping stones, he waded slowly knee-deep across the golden gravel bed of the stream. The water gushed into his boots and he savoured the coolness of the water on his tortured feet.

A scruffy long-haired monster of a dog squeezed out from beneath one of the nearest wagons. It stood on the bank, watching him from behind the shaggy curtain of hair which concealed its eyes. Not until Matt had squelched out of the creek and stood dripping did it condescend to yawn, then amble over to sniff at him.

"Hi, dog . . . how ya doin'?" Matt asked. "Where is everybody, eh?" The dog raised its head and the fringe of hair parted, displaying one eye of brown and the other pale blue. "Well, ya ain't exactly what I'd call ferocious. That right?" With supreme effort the mongrel slowly wagged the tip of his great flag tail and, as Matt walked on, followed with an ungainly ambling gait.

Passing between the nearest two wagons, he suddenly discovered where everyone was.

"Oh Christ," he groaned. "A funeral." With great relief he dumped his load on the grass by one of the wagon wheels.

Flexing his fingers and rubbing at his shoulder, he looked down at the dog. "You look out for me, will ya?" he said. The dog came close, sat, then begged until Matt patted him. "Maybe later, pal. I've things t' do right now."

Malone removed his hat and moved in close at the back of the crowd just in time to hear some preacher say in a flat voice, "Ashes to ashes, and dust to dust . . . amen." In a chorus the rest of the folks echoed the amen, and Malone heard the soil begin to rattle down on to the coffin lid as shovels began to work.

People dispersed, some in embarrassed silence, others talking in awkward whispers. No one seemed to realize Matt was there. Soon he was able to see the men wielding the shovels. To his surprise he saw two graves, but the dirt was only being shovelled back into one.

"Two of you folks died?" Matt asked a middle-aged man in a black, dude suit. The man turned, frowned then looked Malone up and down.

"Not yet there ain't, stranger."

"Oh. Someone's mighty sick then?"

"No . . . but he sure will be." The dude gave a wry grin. "When he gets a rope around his neck," he continued, pointing a fat, stubby forefinger at Malone's feet. "Your pants an' boots . . . they're dripping wet."

"Yeah, I know . . . I'm in 'em."

"What you doing here mister?" The voice was deep, manly and authoritative. "How did you arrive, and what do you want, eh?"

Matt confronted a big distinguished, grey-haired, ex-military-type, sporting bushy white side-whiskers on a weathered face. A heavy gold watch-chain draped across an ample belly, and in his great ham of a fist he held a cavalry-style Colt. The muzzle pointed right at Matt.

Malone raised a quizzical eyebrow at the threatening weapon.

"Now that ain't very friendly, is it?"

"Stranger," the other began, "right

now, I don't feel very friendly." The barrel of the Colt jerked impatiently. "Better humour me. Now!" To emphasize his point he thumbed the hammer back. "I ain't ever been known as a patient man."

"Walked in," Malone answered grudgingly, at the same time pointing with his thumb. "If ya take a gander over there, by the hairy mutt, you'll see my saddle an' stuff."

The big guy spied the empty holster at Matt's side.

"Where's your handgun?"

"Had a run-in with a Sioux war party. Lost it when my horse went down."

People who had already moved away from the site of the burial, pricked up their ears then drifted back, gathering round to listen and satisfy their curiosity.

"Sioux . . . them's Indians?" one of the easterner bystanders interjected. "That's one o' them Indian tribes I heard about back east." Excitedly he explained and pointed out to the others. "If he's been chased an' attacked by Indians . . . " His eyes bulged and he looked around fearfully. "Them redskins could be out there right now . . . just waitin' to murder us in our beds." As the rest of the group began to murmur, he called to Matt, "Hey, mister, them redskins still followin' you?"

"All right Mister Walker," answered the man with the side-whiskers. "Pipe down and stop stirrin' folks up. No call to get your pants on backwards; I'm in charge here, so I'll be doin' the questioning, if you don't mind."

"But, Major, that stranger, he said . . . Indians!" Walker persisted.

"I know that . . . I ain't deaf," the big man scowled then turned his attention back to Malone. "Now where in tarnation was I? Oh yeah, you said you got away . . . without a gun." His words were full of doubt. "And no horse . . . carryin' your saddle and stuff on your ownsome?"

"Had to do me some killin'. It wasn't too easy. After that, I walked all night." Matt stuck his thumbs in the front of his gunbelt. "Please yourself if you believe me or not. 'Cos, Mister who-ever-y'are . . . I just don't happen t' give a shit what ya believe."

Some women in the crowd gave out gasps of disgust and their menfolk felt obliged to mutter condemnation of the strong language he had used. But the steely-grey eyes of the guy holding the Colt never flickered. Instead, they stared right back at Malone in silence for a second or two.

Then everything changed. The side-whiskers lifted a little and the edges of his eyes crinkled as he broke into a grin, uncocked the pistol, returned it to its holster and held out his hand.

"Mortimer. Major Clifford Mortimer. I'm head man on this here wagon train," he announced confidently stepping forward. The handshake came close to bone-crushing in the firmness stakes, but if he had expected Matt to wilt, he was mistaken.

"Malone. Matt Malone." His hand returned the pressure and by mutual understanding they let go and grinned.

"Well, Malone, I've still got a duty to perform," the major mentioned. "I'd like to have another talk. Maybe put a proposition to you when I'm through with it. Right?"

"Uh-huh, I'll listen, but I ain't promisin' anythin'. Understand?"

"Fair enough," the Major agreed, starting to move away through the parting crowd. "Comin' for a look-see?" Without waiting for an answer he strode off. Wondering, Malone followed on.

One wagon had been drawn up close to the base of a giant oak tree. The tailboard's side chains had been unhooked then it had been let down level, its edge resting on the end of a six-inch thick log. A gaunt, weasel-faced man, pale, unshaven and scared stiff, stood on the backboard. His arms had been bound securely to his sides

28

and his spindle legs tied together at the knees.

Above him, a new hemp rope dangled from where it had been thrown over a substantial branch of the oak. The end of the rope had been carefully fashioned into a hangman's noose. Malone watched as the noose was placed limply around the dirt-encrusted neck, and the slip-knot positioned so that it lay alongside the prisoner's left ear.

Another rope, attached to the log supporting the tailboard, was already held by a line of men who stood quietly waiting, looking nervous and just as pale as the prisoner.

"What's this all about?" Matt asked the man nearest to him, as men women and children not directly concerned in the proceedings, formed a circle. "Who is he?"

"Him? That's Hank Smith. He attempted to rob us last night. The bastard gunned down the fella we just buried, in cold blood."

"But hell, fella. What about a trial? Every man's due that at least."

"Mister, that murdering swine had a trial this mornin'. A proper trial," a plain-looking woman with a babe in her arms and an older child tugging at her skirts, informed him. "And that's a lot more than he gave poor Mrs Franklin's husband." Discreetly she directed a finger across to the other side of the circle. "That's her over there."

Malone saw an elegant woman, clad in funeral black, waiting poised with her chin held high, and her gaze fixed sadly but unblinking on the condemned man.

At that moment Major Mortimer signalled for the slack to be taken up on the noose. The other man on the wagon adjusted the slip-knot, drew it closer to the ear and stepped back to safety off the tailboard. In the expectant silence which followed, there came the sound of splashing as the prisoner flooded his pants, and the tailboard dripped urine on to the grass below.

"Hank Smith," the major began in a parade-ground voice. "You have been duly and fairly tried, in front of witnesses, and a jury, all sworn in on the Good Book. Each and every one of them have found you guilty of the heinous crime of murder." He paused to clear his throat before continuing. "Your punishment is to be that laid down in law. You are to hang by the neck until you are dead." Again he cleared his throat. "Before we carry out the sentence, is there anything you wish to say?"

"Yeah, you bastards'll all die. Wait 'til my brothers find out what you've done," the prisoner screamed as he wept unashamedly. "They know where I am, you'll see. An' when they find out what you're all doin', they'll hunt ya down an' slaughter the whole damned lot of ya."

The major glanced over to the men holding the rope to the log. They tensed and adjusted their grips. Then, having received his curt nod, they heaved together. The log pulled away and the wagon's unchained tailboard pivoted down, falling with a resounding crash.

A gasp of horror went up from some of the watchers as Hank Smith's screams were cut off. He jerked then bounced on the end of the rope. His toes turned up and his head twisted grotesquely to one side. Then as he swung, the twist of the hempen strands caused him to spin slowly, limp, like a rag doll on a washing-line.

* * *

"I don't mind tellin' you Matt, as wagon master of this outfit, I'm in a bit of a fix," Major Mortimer admitted. "That man we just hanged, he killed an Englishman I'd hired to act as our scout and meat hunter for the whole trip through to Oregon."

Suddenly he smacked his fist into the palm of his other hand. "Damn, I could kick myself, me being taken

32

in by Smith like that. He rode in the other day and asked if he could tag along with us until we get through the South Pass. Said he felt safer in a crowd." Mortimer shrugged. "I thought an extra gunhand would be useful if we had an Indian attack. So I let him stay."

He picked up the fire-blackened enamel coffee pot then poured out another mug. After a couple of sips he shook his head and sighed.

"Used t' pride myself I could read men."

"There ain't a man born who hasn't been made a fool of at some time or another," Malone consoled him. "It's even worse when it's a woman who fools ya. And I'll bet I've been taken in by more females . . . and more often than you, Major. And I ain't boastin' either."

"Oh I've had my share of woman troubles in my time," the major conceded. "But a lot of women are like that . . . devious." For a moment he stopped to think. "Talkin' of woman trouble. Greg Franklin — the murdered man — he had two wagons. His wife can handle one on her own. Great. But her boy, he's only ten so he isn't a whole heap of use to her when it comes to handlin' a team. If she can't get anyone to drive the other rig, she's goin' to have to leave one good-as-new conestoga behind, along with most of what she owns in this world."

He stopped talking and stared hopefully at Matt who sat up, shaking his head decisively and holding up his hand in protest.

"Oh no, not me. I ain't no wet nurse for no widow woman and a snotty-nosed kid."

"She's not a mean woman. She'd pay you handsomely, I'm sure of that."

"I don't care. No. I won't." Matt Malone stood and went to climb down from the rear of the wagon.

"In that case, you're goin' to have to walk wherever you're headin' for . . . on your own two feet."

The major's words struck home. Matt paused, his foot still on the spring hanger. He considered the last statement and recalled what it was like. Carrying his saddle all that way would be no fun. He twisted his neck to speak to the wagon master.

"What would ya call, bein' paid . . . handsomely, eh?"

"Well, I couldn't rightly say, but she ain't a mean woman."

Malone resumed his climb to the ground.

"And I'd pay you two hundred dollars in gold at the end of the trip," the major called out. "If you do the meat huntin' for us."

Malone climbed back on board.

"Two hundred?"

"In gold . . . guaranteed."

"Tell me where I find this widda woman."

Wreathed in smiles, pleased he had won, Major Mortimer grabbed his hat and prepared to leave his conestoga.

"I'll do better than that, I'll take

you t' see her myself." His great paw clapped Matt on the back. "You'll never regret it. She's a real fine lady and cooks like an angel."

★ ★ ★

Later that same day when the wagons formed up for night camp, the major came along to speak with Malone as he helped Mrs Franklin with her team.

"Some of the womenfolk tell me they're short on meat. I guess this is where you start to earn your pay."

Matt finished unhitching the team and, before taking them over to the night line, posed a question.

"On foot . . . and without a gun?"

"You can have Smith's horse. From now on it's yours," the major answered, "So that's no problem."

Mrs Franklin came up to Matt.

"You may as well have Gregory's gun," she offered. "It's English . . . top quality and hand tooled. My husband thought highly of it."

"I don't know, ma'am," he told her doubtfully. "I can't pay you anything right now. I'd have t' owe ya."

She shook her head.

"I want nothing. It's a gift."

"You can take it out of my wages," he suggested, but she merely shook her head again.

"I don't want it. You'll be doing me a favour, taking it off my hands, Mr Malone." She turned away, her voice breaking a little. "It has too many memories for me."

Major Mortimer coughed, then said gruffly, "That's soon settled then, and you can have Smith's pistol too. Come around and get 'em."

After he'd seen to the immediate chores, Matt stood outside the widow's conestoga and rapped with his knuckles on the footboard.

"It's Mr Malone, Momma," the boy shouted when he had poked his head out through the canvas curtains.

"Climb aboard Mr Malone," she called out. "It's all ready for you."

Immediately he saw the highly polished leather case, he instinctively knew it contained no ordinary weapon. With excitement mounting within him, his thumbs clicked back the catches and lifted the lid.

Hand-engraved Damascus barrels, a perfectly carved and finished butt of walnut burr, along with an inlaid forepiece, nestled snugly in plush green baize. In the other fitted compartments were cartridge loading tools, bullet moulds, ebony and brass cleaning rods, and a leather-backed notebook.

"Sweet Jesus," he breathed to himself, overawed by the quality of the workmanship. "Oh boy!"

"You like it?" she asked simply.

"Like it? . . . Hey, lady. I can't believe it. A man would kill for a dandy gun like this." Reverently he took the pieces from the case and expertly snapped them together. "It feels slick as silk. Kinda heavy though, for a twelve-gauge, and I'll be damned, it's got proper sights." He shook his head in dismay. "No ma'am, I ain't ever seen any shot-gun with sights."

"Oh, that's no ordinary shot-gun," she smiled, quick to correct him. "In fact it's not a shot-gun at all. My husband used to hunt with that when he was stationed in India. A maharajah presented him with it for saving his son's life. You'll find that each barrel is fully rifled. That's an elephant gun you're holding. It'll kill any mortal creature on this earth." Indicating the book in the case, she suggested, "Take a look in there, if you don't believe me."

Dumbfounded he flicked at random through the pages.

"Elephant . . . tigers . . . water buffalo . . . Hecky-me! Yeah, I believe you all right."

"There's a satchel of ammunition, a saddle holster and a whole load of other stuff for it by the driving seat. Oh yes, and a box of .22 bullets as well."

"Twenty-twos?" Matt twisted his face, puzzled. "What're they for?"

"The third barrel, underneath, between the main ones. That's intended for killing small game, birds and things; doesn't make a mess of them for the pot." Taking the gun from him she demonstrated without fuss. "You'll find the small bore's really handy at times."

Matt Malone had never been one to accept a hand-out gratefully, but the spontaneous gift of that gun had him thanking her like a schoolboy being given his first real horse.

"No need for all of that, Mister Malone," she smiled kindly. "All I ask is that you take good care of it, as my late husband would have done."

"You bet I will, lady," he promised, meaning every word. "Heck, ma'am, I ain't ever known anybody who's got, or even seen . . . an *elephant gun*."

3

JUDE SMITH rode on ahead of the others. With no more than a cursory glance at the recent wheel ruts and flattened grass, he pulled up his quarter-bred grey. Sliding from the saddle, he limped stiffly towards the ring of rocks surrounding the cold wood-ash remains of the camp-fire in the centre of the clearing. He crouched and felt at the ashes.

"Them wagons can't be more'n a couple o' days ahead of us, maybe less." One by one he began overturning the smoke-stained rocks, visibly growing more angry with each one, while the other five in the gang dismounted and watched him.

"Has he left a message?" Adam, the second brother, asked, twisting his face and rubbing his backside with his hands to ease it after a day in the saddle.

41

"Does it look like it?" Jude sneered, checking under the last stone before easing himself upright again. "That dang-blasted, no-account young pup!" He began to bang his fist into his other palm as he spoke. "If I've told him once, I've told him a dozen times, t' keep me in the picture."

"Wouldn't worry none; ya know what Hank's like," Adam reasoned. "If that young'un gets the sniff of some woman's drawers he plumb forgets everythin' 'til he's too shagged out t' walk."

The others laughed but Jude's mood was as black as the week's growth of whiskers on his chin.

"If I find out that's the reason for him not leavin' a message," he snarled, clenching and unclenching his fists, "I'll kick his friggin' arse so hard, it'll take a month for the doc t' dig my spurs out."

"Maybe you'd cool him down better, makin' him into a steer, tyin' off his balls like a bull calfs?" Abe, the other brother suggested, winking at the rest. "It sure works for cattle."

"You shut ya damned fool mouth, Abe. I'm boss-man around here, an' ya know how I hate not knowin' what's goin' on." He shouted to the other members of the gang, waving his arms to emphasize his words. "Come on, why ya standin' there? Move! Get the lead out of yer pants. We've some catchin' up t' do and I aim for an early start."

Sullenly the gang set about the normal chores of a night camp. Some collected firewood, while others looked to the needs of the horses, lit a fire or prepared food and the coffee pot.

"Hey, Jude!" The shout, loud and urgent, came from one of the firewood collectors on the far side of the clearing. "Jude. Over here. Better get over here an' take a look."

Sensing trouble, everybody hurried across to see what all the rumpus was about.

"Now what the friggin' hell's the

problem," Jude swore, stomping up to the caller. "Next, you'll be expectin' me t' wipe yer . . . " His words died on his lips as he stopped at the foot of the new graves. His eyes flickered over the words carved on pieces of board nailed to simple crosses.

"Holy shit!" was all he said. Then oblivious to those round him, he sat on his heels, his head in his hands, his shoulders shaking with silent sobs.

"What's it say, Abe?" The one called Tex asked quietly. "What's wrong with Jude, he looks all shook up?"

"This one here" — Abe swallowed hard and began to read aloud — "it says 'Hank Smith, hanged for the cowardly murder of Gregory Franklin'." He choked up and had to swallow some more before saying, "My kid brother . . . they've gone an' killed him."

"Well, what'll happen now, ya reckon?" the latest and youngest recruit to the gang dared to murmur from the side of his mouth to the one named Wilber.

"The Smith boys cling together like a bunch o' grapes. Now, they've lost family." Old Wilbur pursed tobacco-stained lips and spat out an old chaw. "Lead's gonna start flyin' thick an' fast," he predicted. "Folks are gonna die . . . it'll be a massacre, boy."

★ ★ ★

During the latter part of each afternoon, the major himself took over the driving of Mary Franklin's second outfit. That way, Malone was able to ride ahead and scout for a suitable overnight camp-site for the wagon train. At the same time he could keep his eyes open for deer or the big-horn sheep which roamed that area.

Each time he discovered game, the sound of the shot from the elephant gun echoed around the mountains like thunder-claps. Malone thrilled at the accuracy and sheer power of the weapon. Wherever he went, he made a point of carrying the notebook. In spare moments he read and reread the neatly pencilled information the late owner had written in it. He learned about weights of powder, uses of the different bullet moulds, and backsight corrections to cover a wide variety of ranges. Checking, he found the notes to be spot-on.

On one particular day he chose a camp-site only a short distance ahead of the train. To avoid backtracking to tell the major, Malone set a marker in the centre of the trail and carried on to hunt an elk he had spotted moving in the distance.

Between the elk and himself, the virgin forest at that place grew thick and tangled. A lesser man would have given it up as impassable. But Matt thrived on challenge. No matter how slow his progress, he would bag that bull elk or die in the attempt.

On foot, leading his horse and ignoring the thorns ripping at his skin, he forced a passage through the sea of undergrowth. For more than an hour he pressed on, stopping only occasionally to climb a tree and check the position of the elusive animal. It had drawn further away, but with the inborn instinct of a true hunter, Matt knew he would make a kill.

Soon the forest thinned out, and there, only 400 yards further up the opposite draw, the elk munched happily at some scrub.

Matt looped the reins over the broken branch of a nearby pine, and then, cupping his hands over the horse's nostrils, whispered to it.

"Quiet, now you hear?" Gently he blew into the velvety nostrils as he'd seen old Indians do. Soft as a shadow, he began the final stalk. Bent almost double, he kept downwind, only moving closer when the bull elk was busily grabbing another mouthful. In between, he froze, still as a stone.

Climbing on to a rock shelf for a clear shot at the animal from above, he lay down and, estimating the range, set the sight on the elephant gun. Resting his elbows on the rock slab, he fought to control his excitement. It was all too easy to suddenly get a dose of *buck fever* and make a hash of a good shot.

Unaware, the bull elk carried on feeding. Matt took his time, bringing the tip of the foresight up the browsing animal's front leg, settling it in line with the lower chest. His finger began to squeeze, slowly, gently.

"Damn!" A distant rifle shot startled both him and the elk. More shots followed, the echoes resounding from peak to peak as a battle went on further back, down the trail.

The elk had gone but Malone no longer cared. Already, he was scrambling back to his horse as fast as his legs would carry him. By now he could make out the differing sounds of other firearms being used, probably by the members of the wagon train.

"Pesky Indians," he raged as he straddled his mount and sent it galloping dangerously back along the track they had opened out. The briars slashed at him, some catching in his buckskins, peeling curls of it from his sleeves and leggings. Several times his cheeks were scratched deep enough to bleed, but he hardly noticed. He was needed back with the others.

Clear of the trees he made better time, taking short cuts he had been prevented from before because of the wind direction and the sight-line of the elk. Out of the woods, the shots sounded much louder. Soon he would run into danger himself unless he took care.

Where the pass bent round a protruding cliff face, he reined in his mount to a slow walk until he could see the trail beyond. Puffs of powder smoke spurted from high up on the escarpment, away to his right.

The bushwhackers had chosen a good spot for their ambush. At that particular point the trail was too narrow for a wagon and team to be turned. The travellers were sitting targets. The whole line of wagons were huddled, helpless behind the first conestoga whose huge longhorned oxen were already down, shot dead in harness, having brought the complete train to a halt.

Malone saw gunfire being returned in plenty from beneath the conestogas, but knew their shooting was not worrying those firing from above. He had to act. Sitting his horse and watching was not helping any.

Quickly backing out of sight, he turned his steed and forced it up the slope to his right, until the tortuous terrain prevented him from riding any further, Unshipping the elephant gun from its saddle holster, he left the panting horse and scrambled up on hands and knees, making for the action.

It was not possible for him to climb above the ambushers. He would have to be content with targets who had as good as, or better, cover than himself.

At seventy yards range from the nearest hostile gunner, Matt hunched down behind an outcrop of red sandstone that had become overgrown with brushwood. Responding to years of habit, he checked the gun, then settled down to relax his muscles and bring his breathing under control, while waiting for his pulse to slow.

★ ★ ★

Tex raised himself to get a better view of the kid who now fired blindly up at the rocks with a pistol from behind the driving seat of the lead wagon.

"Watch this, Wilber," he called to the old-timer ten yards further along the edge of the ridge. "Bet ya a dollar I take that kid clean between the eyes."

Wilber lifted his head to see where Tex was pointing his carbine.

"Huh, a dollar," he exclaimed in disgust. "Not on your life. A blind man could hit that boy with a piece o' rock."

Tex said no more. Instead, he lined up his sights ready, and breathed easily until the excited kid showed himself again. He waited grinning, as the kid, holding the single-action pistol in both hands, shut his eyes, struggling to apply enough pressure to work the trigger.

A thunderclap reverberated through the air. Tex sprang upright like an uncoiled spring, his reflex action flinging his Winchester out into space. Then, before the first echo, he twisted as he tumbled forward across the rock, and over the edge.

Down below, the kid with the smoking revolver yelled as he watched Tex's body bouncing off the rocks he struck on the way down.

"Ma! Ma! I got me one. I got one."

"Hey, Jude!" Wilber shouted the warning at the top of his voice. "We've got company up here."

"Yeah," Jude yelled back. "Sounded like a big Sharps usin' a double charge. Anybody hit?"

"Just Tex . . . he's had it. Got half his stupid head blowed off his shoulders."

"Well, you forget about the wagons," Jude ordered during the ensuing lull. "Them folks down there, ain't goin' no place. You move on out, and see if ya can nail that sneakin' bastard, before he plugs any more of us."

* * *

Malone had half expected to be shooting at Indians, but instead, had discovered a white man in his sights. It made no difference. Killing any man was pretty much the same, no matter what his colour.

As soon as Tex had taken his involuntary dive over the edge, Matt swivelled his gun muzzle slightly to the right, seeking the next target. The shooting from the bushwhackers had died down. For a time he listened to their excited shouting, noting with satisfaction the hint of hysteria. He smiled, cradled the gun-butt snugly against his cheek, and waited.

If the battered stetson had not

moved, Matt would never have known it was there; its colour merged with the rock. But it did move, and he prepared to fire again.

Slowly the hat travelled along, betraying the position of the wearer behind the weathered sandstone. Matt noticed a gap in the rippled stone formation, where subsidence had caused a shoulder-width V-shaped crack. This was only a yard ahead of the stetson. He sighted his gun on the opening and soon a head came into view.

The recoil rippled through Matt's body, from his shoulder through to the soles of his boots, and another thunderclap shook the surrounding mountains. The head vanished from behind the gap. It was likely to have left the body too, Matt mused grimly.

Breaking the barrels, he withdrew the empty brass cartridge cases, and replaced them in his bandolier for future refilling. All was silent as he reloaded the breech with two more solid-nosed cartridges.

"Wilber?" Malone heard someone call. There was no answer.

"Mmm," Malone muttered to himself. "I reckon I just killed me a Wilber."

The shooting had stopped altogether as both sides waited, wondering what the other's next move was going to be.

"Sam?"

"Yeah, I'm here, Jude."

"You see anythin'?"

"Nope!"

"Well take a g'damned look," Jude ordered, his anger strong and clear.

"You think I'm crazy?" Sam's voice was derisive in the extreme. "Oh no . . . not me, fella. I ain't gonna poke my head out t' have it shot t' hell. No sir, not for nobody."

Matt swung his gun, altering his point of aim to cover a jumble of rocks and bushes a few yards further away, where he estimated the last speaker would be concealed.

"Well, there's one fella among 'em lucky enough t' have a lick of sense," he muttered wryly, thumbing the double curved snake-like hammers all the way back. "But I've a feelin' his luck's just about comin' to the end of the line."

"Sam," Jude called again, seemingly from a little further away than before. "I've warned you 'bout smart-mouthin' me." The words from the frustrated gang leader showed his tension. "Do as ah say . . . or you're on your friggin' own. So chew on that!"

Malone waited for Sam's answer, but the outlaw never made one. The minutes dragged into an hour. All was still except for the rustling, waving seedheads of yellowing grass as the early evening breeze began to blow along the pass.

Something buzzed by close to his ear and a moth landed heavily on the engraved steel rib between the barrels of the twelve-gauge. Relieved it had been nothing more dangerous, Matt watched as it began to walk along towards his face, fluttering its wings as if to keep its balance on the smooth blued steel.

The moth had just about arrived at the point where the hammers normally rested. A couple of scared ptarmigans clattered as they sprang into the air and flew away fast, downwind. Simultaneously, a surge of horses' hooves galloping along, higher up, he knew the survivors of the gang had escaped, although the riders were concealed by the stand of trees growing along the ridge above.

"Hey, you bastards!" Sam stood for a forgetful moment, yelling after the disappearing sounds, and started to run to where his horse was stashed for safety. "Wait. Wait f' me."

Malone reacted. He fired the right-hand barrel, its hammer squashing the fat body of the moth, leaving its frantic wings beating in its death throes for only a split second after the elephant gun had bucked and roared.

The Winchester was flung into the bushes as Sam's arms lifted up, fingers outstretched as if to claw at the clouding sky. His own impetus, helped along by that of the striking bullet, caused him to take two more rubber-leg strides. The hunk of soft lead drove in, heaving him forward as it flattened high up on his spine. Continuing through, it emerged below his throat, from an ugly wound the size of a man's fist. Even before he went down, the nearest rocks in the outlaw's path already showed a scarlet fan of spattered blood.

Then the first fly settled on his corpse, quick to take advantage for her future brood.

After all had returned to silence once again, Matt waited and watched, in case the galloping horses had been a ruse to catch him off guard, when finally, stepping out from cover, he alone stood alive on the ridge.

★ ★ ★

"You all right, Malone?" the major asked when he and a couple of other men eventually arrived up on the ridge to take a look.

"Yeah, I'm in better condition than the others you'll find." He nodded back along the edge. "Back there, in among the rocks."

"That's what I figured when I heard that double-barrelled cannon of yours goin' off," the wagon master grinned. "You don't seem to miss much with that, do you?"

"Can't afford to," Matt admitted, carefully backtracking the outlaws who had left on horseback. "Have ya seen the size of the shells?"

In a dip between some overcrowded ash trees, Malone found what he had been searching for. Taking his time he shuffled along, checked and double checked the iron-shod hoof prints until he was certain.

"By my reckonin', six horses left this way," he remarked to the major. "Three with riders up in the saddle, the others runnin' light."

"So, at least now we know how many

there's likely to be, if they decide to make another call on us."

"Perhaps. On the other hand, we don't know if that was the whole of their outfit," Matt reasoned. "For all we know, they could have a small army of gunhands stashed away in some hideout close by."

"Well we can't afford many of these skirmishes," Major Mortimer sighed. "We're running out of men. We've two more dead down below. Both leavin' widows and kids."

Malone patted his gun.

"Don't you fret none. This'll be ready for 'em."

4

"**I** WISH we'd never laid eyes on that damned wagon train," Adam Smith moaned to his brothers. "First we lose young Hank and then Tex an' Wilber along with that new kid."

"Yeah," Abe went along with him. "Same here." He shook his head as he spoke to the eldest in the family. "Jude, ya didn't ought t've sent Hank along on his own. He never was one for doin' things without one of us ridin' herd to tell him what t' do."

"A fella can't be wet-nursed all his life," Jude snarled back, his temper flaring. "It was high time that boy stood on his own two feet. Hell, it ain't my fault he made a balls o' things by killin' that guy. And it wasn't me who hanged him, was it, eh?"

Getting no immediate answer, he

noisily scraped the remains of his bacon and beans on to the camp fire, afterwards wiping his plate clean with a handful of dry grass. Then he stabbed his hunting knife several times, savagely, deep into the sandy earth.

"It was too much for him t' handle. Responsibility . . . it wasn't for him," Abe insisted. "Ya should've knowed, same as we did."

"Listen! It should've been a simple enough job." Jude glared as he pointed the blade at each of the others in turn. "If Hank had only done what he was supposed to, no more, no less, he'd be sittin' right here with us now. I've always looked out for that boy . . . just like I promised Mama when she was a-dyin'." He stared hard at his two brothers. "Just like I've looked out for you two." He paused expecting an answer but none came. "Well . . . ain't that right?"

"Suppose so," Adam admitted grudgingly.

"An' what d'you say?" Jude glared at Abe.

"Yeah. All right," Abe agreed testily. "What ya said. It's true enough, but . . ."

"But?" Jude's eyes flashed, then narrowed. "But what?"

"Nothin'."

Jude moved in surprisingly swiftly on Abe. His free hand gripped the younger man's shirtfront, twisting the denim in one continuous movement as he hauled him close, face to face.

"What ya mean . . . nothin'?" Provocatively he tapped the flat of the knife blade against the side of Abe's chin. "Ya must've had somethin' in mind? Some little maggot or other eatin' away at that pea-brain o' yours. What was it?"

"I was thinkin', that's all."

"Thinkin'?" Jude spoke quietly but ominously. "Well tell me about it. Tell Adam an' me." He twisted the knife until the edge of the blade threatened to cut into flesh. "We're waitin', we want t' know," he persisted. "We need t' know. Now."

Slowly, Abe pulled his head back, easing away from the pressure of the knife. His face had drained of colour and his mouth hung open.

"It was Hank I was thinkin' about. We haven't got even for him yet."

"Ya think I've forgotten?" Jude pushed his brother away and released his grasp. "Well, that's just where you're wrong, boy. Hank was kin. I won't ever forget. And I'll tell ya somethin' else." He wagged his knife in the air to emphasize his words. "Ah swear on Ma's grave, I aim t' make them travellin' with that train . . . every man, woman an' child of 'em, pay for what's been done. Every one of 'em. Ya hear?"

"Yeah, I hear ya. But when?" Adam demanded. "That's what I'm hankerin' t' know."

"Hey! Slow down. Remember, there's only the three of us left now," Abe protested. "We ain't even got us a proper gang anymore."

"Then we'll get a gang." Jude spun round. "Hell, when's that ever stopped us?" He stared intently at the others, at the same time slipping the knife safely back into its sheath. "If we ain't got somethin', we always go out an' get it, don't we?"

★ ★ ★

The funerals of the two family men, shot by the bushwhackers, had set a depressing tone to the start of the day following the ambush. Major Mortimer had replaced the dead oxen by using his overall authority as wagon master, to commandeer animals from different teams.

"I know it's going to slow us down a mite," he explained to Malone as they were about to move on out again. "But what else could I do? I couldn't just tell that lady to leave her wagon at the side of the trail, now could I?"

"Especially as her old man got

himself shot at the same time as their team," Matt pointed out. "Let's hope we don't have to split 'em up any more, or we'll never make the end of the pass before the snows get here."

Each day a different wagon took a turn at being the one to lead the train. And, at the end of each uneventful day's travel, the driver of the lead wagon would heave a sigh of relief and thank the Lord the bushwhackers had not struck again.

The trail through the pass grew steeper, more rugged and at times, so narrow that it became almost impassable. As the wagons climbed higher the temperature dropped markedly. The need for the train to press on became more urgent. At night, heavy hoarfrost settled on everything, coating the wagons until they looked like sugared cakes. The mornings became miserable for everyone. Only after the fires had been lit and the coffee flowed freely, did people begin to smile and want to socialize again.

Malone's work grew progressively more difficult, as supplying enough meat for the travellers took him further afield. Big game had become scarce, as the animals' natural food supply dwindled. Hunger had driven them further downhill, away from the threat of early winter snows. Even below the higher tree-line, the feeding was better, while down in the valleys, the tall timber afforded more shelter from the cold as well as cover from hungry predators.

Sunday had been ordained, by majority vote, as a time of rest for the travellers, but not for Matt Malone. One such day, food stocks being low, he had ridden out on a hunt at daybreak. During the previous night there had been an extra hard frost, followed by a light dusting of snow. As luck would have it, still within sight of the wagon train he came across the unmistakable tracks of a fully grown stag. Gently he walked his horse in the same direction taken by the deer, keeping quiet and constantly alert for any movement in front.

After about a mile moving steadily downhill, he heard running water and soon broke through the bushes to emerge on to a steeply sloping bank of a cascading stream. Twenty-five yards further on was the animal he had been tracking.

The white-tailed stag was bigger than most he had seen. However, this one was different. It hung, strung forlornly by its back legs, from the lower branch of a tree. Its belly had already been expertly slit from ribcage to anus, opened wide and eviscerated. Below, on the snow-clad frozen earth beneath the animal's head, the pile of offal and guts still steamed in the chilled air as the last drops of blood drained from its cut throat.

Around the unfortunate deer were gathered a hunting party of Shoshoni braves, each ravenously stuffing pieces of the raw liver, still warm and dripping blood, into their mouths as fast as they could chew and swallow.

A few yards further along the river bank, scraggy Indian ponies stood, heads down, snuffling into the yellowed grass under the bushes. Suddenly, before Malone could back his mount quietly into the trees, a pinto with a half-moon painted in blue on its white rump, raised its head high. The inquisitive ears twitched forward, as it gazed across to Matt's mount. Then it snickered.

Malone's horse perked up, loudly neighing an immediate answer, causing the only Indian who faced his way, to look up. The brave's jaws stopped chewing as he stared, frowned, then after what seemed like a year, opened his mouth to gurgle out an almost incoherent warning. At the same time he pointed his blood-stained skinning knife directly at him.

"Holy shit." Matt spat the words out. His mind vividly pictured the last time he and other members of the Indian nations had crossed paths.

He had no desire to wait for an invitation to join in the celebrations. Neck-reining hard and leaning into the turn, he wheeled his mount, plunging back into the meagre shelter offered by the woods.

Before he had travelled far, wild yelps and excited whoops from behind told him that the braves had already mounted and were giving chase. Ducking low in the saddle, Matt hoped to avoid low branches and make himself less of a target for flying arrows. To further confound the aim of his pursuers, he weaved a deliberately erratic course between the trees. Keeping his horse at the gallop, uphill over the hard frozen earth, Matt thanked his lucky stars that on this occasion he had no awkward packhorse to hold him back.

The chase had already gone half a mile. His horse began to blow hard, wheezing and steaming as it sweated from the constant all-out effort Malone had subjected it to. He had demanded far too much of the animal and realized it would never reach the wagon trail without a rest.

Stealing a glance over his shoulder he saw the Indians gradually closing on him. They no longer yelled but showed just as much determination to lift an extra scalp.

Through the trees away to his left, Matt noticed the ground steepened into a cliff face, at the bottom of which mounds or rocks had tumbled down from the mountain heights above. Quickly making up his mind, he changed direction and drove his flagging mount towards the rockfall. Reaching the first of the scattered rock piles he leaped from the saddle, grabbed the twelve-gauge and released his horse. Then running up and over the mound, with his heart thumping wildly in his chest and his breath coming in gasps, he dived down on the other side, behind cover.

The first of the Shoshoni braves, confident in his own victory, rode right up, forcing his pony to scramble on to the rocks, his face a picture of triumph as he looked down, his bone-tipped lance held high, ready for the kill.

The big-bored elephant gun swung up easily in a single fluid movement, as though it was part of Malone. Before the redskin's lance could begin its downward thrust, the thunder of the shot roared with painful intensity.

The heavy ball-nosed lead slug drove in under the raised arm lifting him clear of his startled pony's back as though plucked off by some unseen giant hand. Then he was gone from sight. His pony, terrified by the blast, reared before it slithered and rolled back from the frost-covered rocks. With its legs flailing, it tumbled directly back into the path of the second animal on the scene.

As the surprised second brave fought to keep his pony upright, Malone swung the foresight on him and fired the other barrel. The brave's face altered to resemble a hammered raw steak, and he too was flung out of sight like a wet rag.

The others in the Shoshoni band were not as foolhardy. They leaped from their horses and scrambled for cover among the rocks or behind some of the thicker-trunked trees. Time was on their side. Only when they were good and ready did they begin to snipe with their arrows. Occasionally, fist-sized rocks were lobbed, forcing Malone to keep a watch skywards, as well as on his immediate surroundings. The flying rocks, each of which was liable to bash his brains out, bothered Malone more than the other weapons.

One of the besiegers, hiding behind an old, lightning-struck tree, possessed a pistol which he fired every now and again, but the bullets never came close enough to be a real worry to Malone. Judging by the time intervals, coupled with the highly visible powder-smoke which hung in a miniature cloud around the bowl of the tree, he guessed the weapon to be a single-shot flintlock.

"Matt, boy," he whispered grimly, as he reloaded the big gun, "this could turn out to be a mighty long, cold day."

A lone arrow sang through the air and clattered harmlessly against the rock on his right, close to his head. Twisting to see where it had come from, he was just in time to see the end of a bow vanish from sight into an opening, thirty yards further along the cliff. He shifted his position by a few feet, readied his double barrel and watched the cleft.

Almost at once he saw the tip of an arrow appear. Then the bow came into sight again, being drawn back by strong brown sinewy arms. Before the Indian could bring it on to target, Matt had squeezed the trigger and the dead man's hands released the arrow harmlessly into the air.

Stones clattered behind Malone. As he turned, another bowstring twanged nearby. A sudden, burning sensation caused him to give an involuntary grunt as an arrow pierced his flesh, glanced off the side of a rib and held there, pinning his buckskins to his side.

The shock of the pain induced his finger to jerk the trigger as he pointed the gun at the archer and emptied the second barrel. The shot went high, wide and to the right, splattering the edge of a rock a mere hand's breadth from the Shoshoni's face, before droning away into the distance like a wailing ghost. In spite of the miss, the closeness of it was sufficient to cause the shaken brave to retreat behind the rocks, instead of following up his attack.

Matt became aware of the sticky wetness inside his shirt. He wondered if he should try and pull the arrow free, but decided not to, in case it caused a greater flow of blood.

More movement among the bushes and trees from several positions at once, caught his eye. Slipping his revolver from its holster he prepared for the worst.

"All right, ya bare-arsed varmints,"

he growled in an angry whisper, his keen eyes flicking from side to side, searching for the next attack. "Ya want me . . . you're gonna have t' pay for the privilege."

Sitting, he broke open the elephant gun and held it across his knees. Then, using only his left hand, he deftly reloaded by feel alone. All the while in his gun-hand the pistol was on full cock and held so as to blast the head off any Indian daring to show himself.

A puff of blue smoke showed that the brave with the flintlock was still there behind the dead tree. Malone ducked and waited, but no bullet struck the rocks or flattened on the cliff behind him. Matt shifted position again and was about to look out when more bullets . . . a hail of them, began to fly in all directions.

"What in damnation?" he began, surprised by the sheer ferocity of the gunfire. Then he sagged with relief and almost laughed as none of the lead came his way.

Elated, the pain in his side temporarily forgotten, he joined in, snapping unaimed shots after the fleeing Shoshoni and he realized what was happening. He laughed as the frantic warriors dashed about grabbing their ponies, then rapidly disappeared downhill among the trees. Only when the hammer of the revolver fell with a dull click on an empty cartridge, did he stop working the trigger. He winced as the pain in his side returned. Shutting his eyes tight, he leaned his back against the slab of rock.

Boot nails scraped close to his head and someone jumped down beside him.

"You hurt bad, Matt?"

Opening one eye, Malone tenderly let his fingers feel at the spot where the arrow protruded. He grimaced.

"Not exactly, Major," Malone confessed. "But I sure as hell know how it feels to be a piece o' knittin' stuck on a needle."

The major crouched down, slipped

Malone's knife from its sheath and gently but firmly nicked all the way around the arrow shaft with it. Then having considered the cut to be deep enough, he bent the wooden shaft until it snapped clean in two.

"Right oh, fella, this is grit your teeth an' smile time." He grinned at Matt. "This is the part I always like best of all."

"Bastard." Malone forced himself to grin in return. Then he gasped out loud. "Jesus . . . ya puttin' that thing in, or takin' it out?"

The major held up the front part of the heavy-tipped and bloodied arrow.

"That's it. All over now. What do you want me t' do with this?"

"Don't ask," Matt warned. "Just get on ya knees an' thank the Lord I ain't shown ya already."

★ ★ ★

With the wound in his side clean and freshly bandaged, Malone sat on the driving seat of Mrs Franklin's number two conestoga. Alongside him, her son watched in admiration as Matt handled the team.

"Tell me what it felt like when the Indian arrow hit you," the boy pleaded.

"Ah heck, Willy, I've told ya a dozen times already. Ya must know how it feels better than me by now."

"I know, but I want to be brave like you. I want to know what to do when it happens to me." He stopped talking and thought for a while, still looking up at Malone's face. "I say, Mr Malone . . . you didn't cry, did you?"

Matt almost burst out laughing at the English accent and the seriousness of the boy's question.

"Hell, no, boy. A growed man don't cry, not for just gettin' himsel' hurt."

"That's what my father says," the boy began, then remembering, corrected himself. "Said when he was alive." Suddenly, silent tears ran down the well-scrubbed freckled cheeks. Embarrassed, he blinked hard and said, "Sorry, I can't help it, sir."

Malone's left arm slipped around Willy's shoulders, then in spite of the action causing his wound to pain, he pulled the lad close in a rough, manly hug. At first the boy resisted, but all at once he gave in to his feelings and began to sob.

"That's right Willy-boy, you go right ahead, let it all out. It don't do any good holdin' grief inside ya."

"But I don't . . . want . . . to cry."

"There ain't nothin' wrong with a growed man sheddin' a few tears," Matt pointed out. "Cryin's all right when the tears are for somebody else. Especially someone who's been kin an' brave as yer pa."

The boy remained snuggled close for a long while. When he did sit up, his tears had dried. In some way Malone could not quite put a finger on, Willy had changed. For a time neither spoke, but sat contentedly, each with his own private thoughts, swaying to the rocking motion of the creaking wagon.

"What's that Mr Malone?"

"Eh, what's what?"

"That noise. Can't you hear it?"

Matt tilted his head and listened.

"It's a sort of rumble," the boy explained, " . . . a bit like thunder or potatoes tumbling down the stairs, or something."

Malone swung the team as close to the cliff face as he could manage, hauled on the reins and slammed on the brake. Then, yelling at the top of his voice and ignoring his wound, he sprang from the wagon and waved directions to the drivers in line behind.

"Avalanche! Get ya outfits into the cliff bottom. Hurry!" Reaching up, he dragged Willy from the seat then pushed him unceremoniously under the conestoga. "Now Willy-boy. You do like I say. Stay there 'til I come an' fetch ya, or I'll whomp yer arse good an' hard."

Malone sprinted back to help the

boy's mother handle her horses which, having sensed the oncoming danger, were plunging and rearing. Even as he wrangled the team, men and women could be heard screaming further back along the line. Glancing up, he watched the first of the spinning boulders cascading down towards the wagon train from the steep mountain slope high above.

5

THE earth and everything around them shook. Beneath the conestoga Malone lay huddled close to the boy's mother, his body halfway over her, holding her down, protecting her from her need to seek her son. The air was a dark fog of choking, freshly-ground stone dust which stung their eyes and filled their nostrils. They could taste it on their tongues and felt it gritting between their teeth.

Barely seventy yards away, behind Mrs Franklin's wagon, things were at their worst. At that place the trail naturally bowed out away from a bulge in the mountainside offering no overhead cover to those below. The horrific scene was like a concentrated artillery bombardment.

Rocks rained down, demolishing the wagons, turning their stout planks into splinters, like exploding shells. Hundreds of tons of earth, snow and uprooted trees poured from above, in a relentless and seemingly continuous stream of destruction. Complete, fully-loaded wagons were crushed and buried. Others were swept out over the edge as discarded garbage, along with their terrified teams.

Whole families had their lives ended, snuffed out with no chance to even call out goodbyes to one another. The avalanche showed neither compassion nor favouritism, but swept on, destroying anything or anyone in its path.

The ground stopped shaking. The noise died away into the distance down the slopes below the trail. As the dust settled, survivors were left coughing, bewildered in the deathly stillness.

Matt let Mrs Franklin go.

"William," her voice was strident with concern as she scrambled out on hands and knees from between the wheels. "William . . . where are you?"

"Under the wagon like I told ya,"

Malone said, crawling out with her. "Ya think the boy's deaf? Give 'im a break and let 'im grow up. There ain't no need t' embarrass the kid, yellin' like that."

Before she could frame a suitable reply to his rudeness, Matt moved off at a trot to give what help he could to the less able survivors of the train. He passed the first wagons, only two of which bore signs of damage, but from there on everything got worse. He came upon horses and oxen lying crippled, struggling on the ground, and grew more and more angry. Drawing his revolver he went from animal to animal, shooting each one to end its misery.

"Come on, all you folks who ain't hurt bad, forget about yer own damned rigs," he demanded at the top of his voice. "Come on and give me a hand t' help them who ain't been as lucky."

Followed by those he had shamed and stung into action Malone clambered to the top of the pile of earth and rock which now effectively blocked the trail behind them. They gazed in awe at the extent of the destruction.

"I can't believe it," Mick McKay, an ex-shopkeeper from St Louis, muttered as he made his way down the other side of the mound along with Matt. "All that damage . . . in such a short time. It don't seem possible somehow."

"It's God's curse for us breakin' His commandments," the dour grey-haired Irishman on his left explained.

"Don't give us any o' that bullshit, Murphy," the first man retorted testily. "What commandment have any of my family broken, eh?"

"'Thou shalt not kill'." Murphy wagged an agitated finger in the other's face, his eyes fierce and gleaming with a pop-eyed lunatic stare. "You've all killed," he sneered. "Every single one of you. Aye, I warned you all at the time you held that ungodly trial. 'Vengeance is mine', sayeth the Lord. I told you how it would turn out, but not one of you sinners took a blind bit of notice." He waved his arm around at the devastation. "This is God's retribution for hanging that poor lamb who strayed off the beaten path."

"Poor lamb, was he?" Jones, a normally meek little bird of a man, chirped up. "Well, I'd still vote t' do it again . . . and I'd volunteer to slip the rope around his murderin' neck, Lord, or no Lord."

★ ★ ★

By nightfall on the day of the disaster, eager teams of men had rescued everyone who was going to be rescued.

Then, by lamplight, the recovered dead had been lined up side by side to share in a communal grave dug a short distance further on, where the trail widened. The wagon master had read words from the Good Book and, as a hymn was sung the grave had been filled in.

The day had been a long one.

Everyone had slogged their guts out, non-stop, but still had not even scratched the surface of all that remained to be done. It would be a week, maybe longer, before the train could unite again and continue on its way.

The major was one of those who had lost their wagons and had moved what kit he had salvaged into Mrs Franklin's second wagon, to share with Malone. At the end of the day of disaster, they strolled together, discussing the problems.

"With a third of the able survivors salvaging the damaged wagons, and everyone else, including the walking wounded, clearing the rockfall from the trail, it's going to be touch an' go. What do you think, Matt?"

Malone pushed his hat to the back of his head and slurped his coffee, shaking the last drops on to the ground before answering.

"Well," he began, "the way I see it, there's some mighty big rocks among that heap. I don't see how we can shift 'em without heavy equipment, or even explosives." Grim-faced, he kicked a stone out over the edge of the track. "I don't like the way the weather's closin' in. It's gettin' colder and snow looks like it's gonna beat us, Major. And if we get caught in that . . . well, ya don't need me t' tell ya what'll happen. You'll lose most, if not everyone, on the train."

The major's shoulders lifted as he heaved a sigh. Looking down he thoughtfully selected a pebble with the toe of his boot, then with a sudden display of frustration, he kicked the stone out into the black void beyond the edge.

"I agree," he stated quietly. "That's exactly how I see things. A decision's got to be made. And I'll have to make it, tonight. The folks here have all staked their money and trust me to get them through. I owe them that much."

Stepping back, away from the edge of the precipice, they ambled back into the circle of firelight, heads down and each deep in his own thoughts.

"Any ideas, Matt?" the major broke in, quietly so that others around the friendly blaze did not hear.

"Uh-huh. A couple."

"Well . . . I ain't too proud to take advice," the major told him. "Why don't you tell me?"

Malone reached down by the fire for the coffee jug and filled his tin mug again, then, pouring some into the major's cup, he nodded.

"All right. This is the way I see it." Squatting down beside the fire, he took a partly burned stick and rubbed the charred end on one of the stones bordering the fire. When he had fashioned a suitable point, he used it as a stylus, and began to scratch a rough drawing on the ground.

The major knelt on one knee, watching each part of the plan unfold, and listening as Malone explained his strategy.

"This is the rockfall, here. Right?"

"Right," the wagon master agreed.

"If we had twice as many men we couldn't shift it in time. So, it seems to me, we should forget about doin' that."

"You want to leave it as it is?"

Malone glanced up at the major, expecting more comment but when there was none, ignored the question.

"I've been checkin' around with the wagon owners," Matt continued. "We've plenty of good strong ropes, blocks an' tackle, axes an' all we need." He waited for a response.

"Uh-huh, OK. So . . . what d'you plan to do with all that stuff?" the major asked. "But don't go around the scenic route, get to the point."

"I say we unload all the serviceable wagons trapped behind the fall, strip the frames and canvas off 'em, remove the wheels, then drag 'em up and over the pile. When that's done, do the same with the animals and everything else."

At first the wagon master made no

reply. He stayed there, looking at the drawing.

"It's one hell of a job you're contemplating, and it'll be dangerous." Deep in thought, he absentmindedly combed his fingers through his side-whiskers, then at last he murmured, "I can see us losing a few men doing that."

"An' we can lose everybody if we don't do somethin' quick," Matt retorted, his patience growing thin. With his jaw set he looked the other man straight in the eye. "Well?"

"All right, Matt. It seems a crazy scheme, but it could work. And I haven't a better idea," the major admitted. "We'll do it your way. We'll haul everything over the top."

While the major organized the men at the wagon train, Malone led a team of men back along the trail then down a less steep part of the mountainside. Their job was to seek out suitable tall and straight timber to fell. This was to be hauled back to construct sheer-legs or to act as skidways on either side of the rockfall.

From dawn to dusk for two days, they chopped, sawed, trimmed and hauled late into the night; only the animals rested. Weary, dirty and cold, men worked on by lamplight, positioning and securing the timber all the way up and over the pile until a continuous skidway of de-barked and wagon-greased logs connected the trail again.

Erecting the sheer-legs was more difficult. At the first attempt to raise them into place, a boulder was dislodged, a lashing gave way, and one of the giant poles slipped, bringing its partner down with it. As it went down, the thick end at the base, kicked back, hitting a helper in the chest, and hurling him from the pile to crash to his death on the rocks below.

When the rope had been threaded through the pulley block at the 'V' where the sheer-legs joined at the top, it was then led down and attached to the team, coupled sixteen-strong, on the other side.

The first naked wagon to be hauled was manhandled, without its wheels, on to the beginning of the skid poles.

"Steady men, keep it straight in line," warned the major. "And you with the ropes, see you make certain sure they'll hold fast."

Satisfied that all was as it should be, he stepped back and looked up at the sheer-legs high above. Lifting his arm, he signalled to Matt on top of the pile.

"Take her away, Malone. She's all yours."

Malone waved an acknowledgement before he turned and whistled to those down below on the other side with the horses. Whips cracked. The team leaned into their collars, and as they moved forward, the slack was taken up until the ropes sang. The stripped-down conestoga resting on its axles, jerked, creaked and groaned in protest, then slowly began its journey up the greasy skids.

Everyone not directly involved in the work gathered to watch the first wagon reach the peak of the mound. When it did, Matt's hand shot up to signal again to the teamsters. Immediately a gang of men set about looping pre-formed cradle ropes over each end of the axles. Then the sheer-legs were pulled upright, lifting the wagon, swinging it over and lowering it on to the skids on the downward slope.

"There ... works like a charm. Didn't ah say it would," a happy Matt boasted to the others as they transferred the tow rope from the front, took it to a snatch-block and secured the end to the rear of the wagon. "Now, careful. Let go; take it nice an' steady."

As the weight came back on to the team below, the whips cracked again. The horses backed steadily, lowering the load smoothly down the skids. When it reached the trail, a cheer went up along with a wave of spontaneous hand clapping. Almost before this had died down, the wheels had been fitted back on and the wagon rolled out of the way.

"Well, that's the first of 'em." Malone grinned with relief. "Right fellas." He clapped his hands together. "Come on, let's get the rest up and over."

★ ★ ★

"I've got to admit," the wagon master began, as the supplies had mounted up on the right side of the pile by noon on the next day. "I never thought we'd pull it off . . . at least not as quickly as we did. You did a hell of a fine job, Matt. You know, you'd have made a first-class officer in the army."

"Me . . . an officer?" Matt flushed and twisted away to hide his embarrassment. "Huh, that's a laugh. I can't abide the idea of givin' stupid orders to folks. Hell, why should I want t' do a fool thing like that? Never could stand takin' orders from anyone in authority, myself." He shook his head vigorously.

"No, sir, that kind of life, it ain't for me."

"You're wrong," the wagon master argued seriously. "In my time I've come across all kinds of men. I understand them. That's how I know you're a natural leader." He smiled warmly. "Have you noticed how the folks around here come and ask you what they should do?" He tapped his finger against his chest. "And I'm the one who's supposed t' be the boss-man." He grinned and delivered a friendly punch to Malone's upper arm. "Hell, if I was a younger man, I'd be jealous enough to buckle on a gunbelt and call you out."

"Mister Malone, sir," Mick McKay butted in. "We're goin' to have to leave three wagons behind. There's three wheels beyond fixin', and they're all different sizes. What'll we do?"

The major laughed.

"See what I mean?" he smirked good-naturedly at Matt. With a theatrical wave of his open hand, he urged, "Go on . . . tell the man."

"I'll come along an' take a look-see," Matt told McKay. "There ain't no way we can afford to lose any more wagons."

Arriving at the crippled vehicles, he went straight into action.

"Right-oh, fellas, this is what ya do."

★ ★ ★

It began to snow heavily the next morning, shortly after Malone, driving the lead wagon, had got the train under way. In spite of the bitterly cold wind, most of the travellers were in high spirits. At last they were on the move again.

At the rear of the train two wagons left continuous furrows in their wake, each having had six-inch diameter tree trunks lashed on, to take the weight and act as skids, in place of the shattered wheels. A third conestoga looked like it had broken its back having a sloping floor due to its normal two large wheels at the back and two foreign, smaller ones on the front axle.

"My mother says you have good ideas, Mr Malone, sir," Willy said honestly and out of the blue, as once more he sat beside his hero.

"Oh yeah?" Malone tried not to show his interest.

"I do too," the boy added. "Mother says that it's likely you have sons like me at home, maybe daughters too." Willy looked at him earnestly, waiting for the answer. When none was forthcoming, he pushed for the information he wanted. "Is she right, sir?"

"No she damn-well ain't . . . an' I ain't married neither."

"Oh, good." Willy brightened more. "I'll let her know. Women like to know these things."

"Oh, expert on women, are yer?" he scowled. "Give my ears a rest, boy," he growled to cover his confusion at the lad's honest but pointed questions.

"Keep them there expert eyes of yours on the road ahead. Could be you'll see somethin' I don't."

Then he settled back with his thoughts. He liked the boy . . . and come to that, his mother too. As he drove on in silence he found himself recalling how she had, on her own initiative, set up a makeshift hospital after the avalanche. How she had cared for the injured, staying awake and by their sides all through the night, comforting and tending to their wounds, stitching them up, fixing broken bones with splints, using her own brand-new bed linen, to tear up as bandages. Doing a load of things most women would never dream of doing.

Yeah, he mused to himself. Ah reckon there's a whole lot of good in that woman. Even if she does talk funny an' acts kind of fancy-like.

"The snow's getting deeper, Mister Malone."

The swirling wind drifted the snow against the side of the pass, piling it high, adding danger, concealing fallen rocks which could easily smash a wheel. The thickly flying flakes obliterated the trail only a short distance ahead, making driving difficult and the work extra heavy for the snorting teams.

Willy's voice brought Matt back with a start.

"Shouldn't we stop and wait 'til it stops?" the boy asked.

Startled out of his musing, when Malone looked up he saw what the boy meant.

"No. Not here. If we stop we might never get started again. We'll have to keep going 'til we get clear of this pass." To himself he added a grim afterthought — if we can.

He unshipped the whip from its stowage before they reached the first of the drifts, and began cracking the lash above the swaying broad backs of the team.

"Yah . . . yah. Yup yup," he yelled above the noise of the flapping canvas wagon cover. "Yah, yah, yah!" The whip cracked harder, the snaking lash stinging the reluctant horses. Lunging forward they broke into a fast trot, using the momentum of the wagon to force through the first of the drifts.

Just when it seemed that the teams had reached the end of their strength, the trail began the descent. The track widened, the depth and frequency of the snow drifts grew less, and, as the altitude reduced, so did the wind and bitter cold. The teams now moved at a steady pace, helped by gravity and the occasional judicious application of the brakes.

Shortly before nightfall Malone led the train out from the gaping maw of the pass. Selecting the first relatively flat ground in the lee of a stand of pines, he pulled up his team and kicking hard, slammed on the brake.

"This'll do for tonight, Willy-boy. Better run along an' see if your ma needs some help with the horses." As the shivering boy hurried away, Malone climbed down stiffly to wave the other wagons into position for the night camp.

"We can't carry on like this, Major," Matt said later as they sat inside the wagon, huddled with plates of hot stew warming their knees. "Winter's set in early this year. We'll have to wait somewhere safe 'til the spring thaw. Besides, there's a hundred an' one things needin fixin' if we aim to make Oregon without losin' any more folks or wagons."

"That's what I've been thinkin' about," the major conceded. "There's an army fort, about twenty miles south of here. When I was a young shavetail lieutenant, I was stationed there for two years, it had one or two silver mines and the makings of a one-horse town growin' alongside."

"Could be a ghost-town by now, but it's worth takin' a chance," Malone mumbled, spooning another mouthful of stew. "Can't be any worse off than we are here. The women an' kids'll appreciate a rest from the trail. It'll mean good shelter, and time to do the work in safety. Folks can buy fresh supplies and maybe the use of a doctor. Could be the last chance they have this side of Oregon."

"Yes, and we could be there in a couple of days easy travellin'. Who knows, the army could still be there. We might even discover there's a blacksmith, and maybe a professional wheelwright to make repairs for us." He stroked at his side-whiskers, his fingers absent-mindedly twisting strands of hair into curls. "And a saloon with a piano and high-kickin' gals with painted lips and lace-trimmed drawers." A smile played on his lips as he began to stroke his whiskers. "Yes . . . I like that idea. That's what we'll do. We'll make a bee-line for there, tomorrow."

6

THE swing doors of the Silver Moon saloon clattered open then noisily banged back. Abe Smith, with flakes of snow still adhering to his dirty yellow slicker, pushed through the draught curtains and hurried into the warmth of the bar room.

"Well, well, look who's just blown in," Adam Smith exclaimed to his elder brother. "Abe's lookin' like he's won a thousand dollar turkey-shoot."

Jude glanced up from his poker hand and peered out from under the wide brim of his hat. Then he dropped his gaze back to consider the hand of cards he had been dealt. Only when Abe had stomped across and stood grinning by his side, did he speak.

"Hi, Abe," Jude greeted him without looking up again. "What's tickled your arse?" he asked laconically as his long slim fingers felt among the pile of poker chips in front of him. "Why ya grinnin' like a damn fool?" Nonchalantly he tossed a century chip on to the others in the kitty. "Raise a hundred," he informed them, looking up at the still silent Abe. "Well? Ya found yourself a new whore who ain't got the clap, or have ya come across somethin' really interestin'?"

The other players around the card table sniggered and watched Abe, awaiting his answer.

"Why don't ya stop smart-mouthin' me an' go outside to take a look?" Abe suggested sullenly, angered by Jude's lack of respect for him in public. "Maybe you'll learn somethin you'll like."

Having said his piece, he spun on his heel, marched over and pushed through the men bunching around the bar.

"Red-eye, Barny," he yelled out to the barman. "Get the lead out an' leave me the bottle handy."

None of the poker players spoke. Instead, they exchanged surprised glances before looking at Jude. Bemused, he hesitated for a moment then, picking up his cards, scraped back his chair and made for the door.

"Hold it a while, boys," he called over his shoulder to the other gamblers, as Adam followed him. "Grab yourselves a drink from my bottle. I'll be back."

Even before he pushed himself out from between the saloon doors and stepped on to the sidewalk, Jude Smith had recalled the sounds.

The snow-caked, battered wagons which rumbled slowly past in front of the saloon were familiar. He recognized one of the outfits, and then another, as those he had seen in front of his gun-sights. His eyes lit up with anticipation.

"Well I'm damned," he muttered aloud. "So we ain't lost 'em after all."

"No wonder Abe was s' full of himself," Adam laughed, looking out over the top of the swing doors. "Seems like we're still in business, eh, Jude?"

"We sure are, but this time we're gonna plan things properly."

Adam stepped outside and sidled close to his brother's shoulder.

"If they've only come t' pick up supplies, they might be movin' on again at first light."

"Don't be stupid," Jude snarled in despair. "Just use yer eyes. A blind mule can see the state them wagons are in. They ain't goin' to be leavin' here 'til they've been all fixed up." Jude slowly shook his head. "No, by my way o' thinkin', I reckon they'll be here 'til the spring thaw."

"So that means we'll have to keep our heads down. As soon as any of them there travellers lay eyes on us three, they'll bring in the law."

"Ah, hell, Adam," Jude remonstrated. "Why don't you ever stop and think before ya open yer mouth? How can any of 'em recognize any of us, eh? We were under cover, shootin' at them.

None of 'em were close enough. How could they 'ave got a good look at us?"

"The guy who shot old Wilber an' Sam, he was up on top of that buff the same as us. He could've seen."

"Listen, stupid, if that guy with the cannon had seen us, d'you think we'd be standin' here, freezin' t' death now?" Jude shook his head again, turning to re-enter the saloon. "No, we'd be dead meat, same as Tex and the others."

"What we gonna do, then . . . nothin'?" an unconvinced Adam asked, following closely behind.

"We do nothin' at all . . . except get t' know them folks. Find out what they've got, that we want more. Same as Hank was supposed t' do." Jude's eyes appeared to glaze over and he seemed to stare into the future. "But he's mine. Whoever he is, I want him . . . that bastard with the big gun."

★ ★ ★

The wagons were camped on the land between the fort and the town. A prudent choice for it kept the womenfolk out of the path of the miners hell-bent on boozing at the Silver Moon or living it up in the whorehouse next door to it.

Later, at the fort, a sentry on the gate challenged Malone and the major, holding them at gun point while he called out for the sergeant of the guard.

"Major Clifford Mortimer, to see your commanding officer," the major stated briskly when the NCO emerged from the warmth of the guardroom, cursing to himself. "And be quick, before we freeze to the marrow."

The craggy, bull-necked sergeant hesitated. Taken aback by the dishevelled state of the wagon master's clothing, yet impressed by his educated speech and manner, he clicked to attention and saluted.

"If you'll follow me, sir."

A few minutes later they waited,

shivering in front of a regulation desk in an office with a dead fire, for the CO to come in. Heavy footsteps sounded along a passageway. When they stopped, the office door opened and a skinny, fair-haired young captain, one of the new breed, entered. He marched to the chair behind the desk and sat down before even looking at his visitors.

"Yes," he snapped out, not even offering his name or his hand. "You wish to speak with me. What about?"

The major turned beetroot-red, and handed his official credentials to the seated despot. The man hardly glanced at them.

"Yes, yes," he snapped out like a terrier. "So you were a major, I know that already; my sergeant told me as much. I suppose you arrived with that tribe of gypsies camping outside the fort? Come along now, why are you here . . . Major?" He emphasized the word 'major' with a barely concealed sneer, as though it was a dirty word.

111

"What's so all hell-fired important that you should disturb me outside normal working hours?"

Major Mortimer kept his temper in check. He breathed deeply and leaned forward, his hands gripping the corner of the desk.

"First of all, I demand the respect due to me and the other civilians out there who pay your wages . . . Captain. Those people are not gypsies. They're Americans who have fired more bullets in anger than you've fired on the shooting range. They're tax-payers; men, women and kids who've fought with Indians. And they've been bush-whacked by desperadoes, and driven them off. Not so many days ago, they were involved with the biggest damned landslide you're ever likely to see. It cost a lot of 'em their kith an' kin. Now a whole heap of them are out there in sore need of a doctor."

"You should have had a doctor with you," the captain put in quickly, determined to be in the right.

"We had. He got himself murdered."

The captain sat up.

"By whom?"

"A young fella, went by the name of Hank Smith. Come t' think of it, he was a mite like you," the major informed him, then corrected himself. "No, he was *a lot* like you. We hanged him . . . all nice and legal, by the rules."

"Oh, so you do use rules?"

"Right down the line. All the way to Washington if necessary. I've got pull there . . . get my drift . . . Captain? Now, I need a loan of the fort sawbones." He grinned. "It's your duty to comply."

From then on, the commanding officer treated him civilly, but with the coldest of good manners. Neither the major nor anyone else belonging to the wagon train, were invited or encouraged to share the facilities of the fort, or the spartan comforts of the officers' mess. Nor were they allowed to utilize any of the artisan skills of the enlisted men.

These troops, the major and Malone were told, were strictly for the aid and protection of a team of government surveyors, engineers and cartographers mapping the territory. The junior officers, fashioned in the same mould as their captain, were just as haughty. Whether by their commanding officer's instructions or their own nature, they kept to themselves.

Only the grey-haired medical officer, long past normal retirement age, and the oldest officer on the post, offered his help and friendship. It so happened that he had known the major from twenty years before, but this did not influence his decision to help. He cared little for authority and would have devoted his time and skill without being ordered.

"The young 'uns in the officers' mess, they ain't what they used to be, Major," he cackled one night as the three of them worked on a bottle of red-eye, after one of his visits. "Not like when you an' me were.

It ain't like a real army any more."
He grinned meaningfully and tapped
his finger on Malone's chest. "That
was when bullets an' war arrows were
a-flying' at us like a hailstorm in a
hurry."

"So, you've seen plenty of action
then, Doc?" Matt queried.

"Yes, indeed I have. Too damned
much, young fella." He paused to have
another swallow of his drink. "I ain't
ever been one for boastin', but . . . "
— leaning closer he winked — "I'll
wager I've dug more hunks of lead
out of men's hides than most of them
miners have dug out of the ground with
picks an' shovels. And that's the gospel
truth of it."

Matt grinned.

"Is that a fact?"

The doctor's eyes opened wide then
closed again as he frowned. "You don't
believe me." Pushing his face close
enough for Matt to get drunk on the
fumes of his breath, the doc grew
more intense. "Listen, son, after I've

operated, I've seen the orderlies gettin' double hernias, from just liftin' the buckets of slugs I'd removed."

Malone was unsure how to handle the situation, but the medical man suddenly laughed and slapped him on the shoulder.

"Got ya goin' that time, didn't I, eh? Didn't know if I was tellin' the truth or lyin', eh? Well . . . I was lyin'. But only just. Them orderlies I was tellin' you about, they mostly used t' get ordinary, single hernias."

★ ★ ★

"There's one of the fellas from the wagon train," Abe warned, digging his elbow in Jude's back as they leaned against the bar of the Silver Moon.

"Who . . . where?"

"The little guy, just come in, by the first table." Abe began to smile. "The one Fat Mary's puttin' the lean on."

Jude leaned his elbows on the bar and watched Fat Mary's sales pitch being performed with the newcomer.

"Looks mightly flustered, don't he?" Jude announced. "I think it's my public duty to go on a mission o' mercy an' rescue that poor defenceless little guy."

Tossing his head back he downed his drink, burped loudly and wiped his mouth on the back of his hand. Then arrogantly he pushed his way through a beer-swilling crowd of barflies. Unworried by their exclamations of protest, he swaggered across to grab the plump brassy blonde's hair with one hand while his other slapped a stinging blow on her ample rump. Jerking on the tresses, he heaved her back, away from the scarlet-faced ex-shopkeeper.

"Go pick on somebody yer own size, Mary," Jude told her, shoving her in the direction of the doors. "Go wait for a big fella, someone who ya wouldn't crush to a pulp."

Flashing a broad smile at McKay, he held out the hand of friendship.

"Hi, I'm Jude Smith. You're new around these parts."

Glad to be saved from Mary's clutches, the rescued man accepted the proffered hand and shook it warmly.

"Mick McKay . . . I'm from the wagon train. Thanks for savin' my hide. That lady had a mighty insistin' way about her." He thumbed towards the bar. "I'd like to buy you a drink, Mister . . . er . . . Smith."

"Call me Jude." Placing his open hand on the other's shoulder he gently but forcefully propelled him to the bar. "Maybe I'll have that drink after, but as the owner of the Silver Moon, I always make it a point to buy the first drink for a stranger myself."

"Now that's mighty neighbourly of you," McKay answered with bright-eyed delight showing in his face. "I can see I'm goin' to like this town, and the folks in it."

In under an hour McKay, helped by the three Smith brothers, was gibbering drunk, and willing to answer any question they cared to put to him.

"I hear tell you had a hangin' somewhere back along the trail," Adam prompted. "That right, Mick, did ya?"

"Sure. The young punk went an' murdered Greg Franklin. He was the doc." Rolling his glazed eyes from face to face, McKay grinned stupidly. "You know somethin'?" He began to laugh. "That yella, murderin' bastard, before we hung him, he pissed his pants . . . in front o' the women an' kids." His laugh grew louder and out of control until tears spilled from his eyes.

Abe clenched his fist and raised it as his anger surged to the surface. Jude saw him and shook his head grimly, warning him to keep cool. Waiting until McKay stopped his fit of laugher, Jude spoke in a quiet coaxing voice.

"Ya sure have had a rough time, Mick. Now ya said there's one of you fellas uses some special kind o' gun?"

"I did?" McKay swayed in his chair, screwed up his eyes and looked puzzled. "I said that?"

"Ya sure did, friend," Jude insisted. "Didn't he boys?"

"Uh-huh, we all heard 'im, but I think it was the booze doin' the talkin'. He was just shootin' his mouth off."

"You shayin' I'm drunk?" Mick McKay tried to stand but Jude placed a restraining hand on his shoulder.

"Steady down, Mick, we're all pals here. I know you ain't drunk an' so do the boys. It's just that they're kind of curious about this guy who uses the big gun ya mentioned."

"We know ya wouldn't lie to us," Adam butted in. "That ain't your style. It's likely we made a mistake when ya mentioned about the gun."

"Yeah," Abe pretended to agree. "Hell, there ain't no such gun."

"That's just where you're wrong, mister," McKay flared. "It's a double-barrelled weapon, and in case ya don't believe me, you go and look up Matt Malone, 'cos he's the fella who owns it." This time when he tried to stand up, no one attempted to prevent him.

He stood there, his hand holding the back of his chair to steady himself. "I'll bet any damned amount ya like to wager. It's true."

"All right," Jude Smith agreed. "I'll take that bet. How about a hundred dollars . . . more if ya like?"

Pure greed glittered in the bloodshot eyes of the drunken ex-shopkeeper. Concentrating hard he worked out his potential profit. Then he struck like a snake.

"Two hundred!"

"You're on," Jude answered just as quickly, "if you can bring that guy and his gun here, inside an hour."

"An hour?" Sudden doubt seemed to sweep through McKay. He gawped, looked from brother to brother, then pleaded, "But what if I can't find 'im inside an hour?"

"He's gonna welsh on the bet, Jude," Abe sneered.

"Yeah, he's backin' down already," Adam joined in with disgust.

"No he ain't," Jude smiled. "Mick's

a man of his word . . . ain't ya Mick?"
He took out his wallet and counted
$200 into a pile on the table. "That's
my money," he said. "Where's yours?"

Colour drained from McKay's face.
His hands desperately tapped each of his
pockets in turn. Then he licked his lips.

"I don't carry that kind of cash on
me. But I can get it," he said quickly.
"It's back on my wagon."

"Then . . . get it." Jude stuck his
thumb in the arm-holes of his vest.
"And bring the guy with his gun
. . . what was his name again?"

"Malone. Matt Malone." Staggering,
he wove a path through the other
drinkers, heading for the swing doors.
"Don't you go away," he called out
loud enough for lots of folks to hear.
"I'll be back . . . in half an hour."

Jude grinned at his brothers.

"Right, boys, out the back way. You
know what t' do."

★ ★ ★

122

Delighted by his shrewdness at raising the bet to double the offered stake, Mick McKay breathed in the cold air outside the saloon. Having stepped on to the boardwalk he set off, stumbling along as fast as rubber legs would permit. His senses swam and he sang happily to himself, head down against the snow which fell steadily, and unaware of the footsteps coming up alongside.

Something hard, delivered with considerable force, struck the back of his skull. As he collapsed, hands grabbed roughly under his arms.

The searing pain inside his nose brought him round. Jerking his head up, he wanted to claw at the cause of his torment, but could not. His hands were held rigid to his sides . . . by rope.

"Told ya he'd not like a hot cigar stub up his nose." Adam's voice drifted through the haze of McKay's eye-watering agony. "Ain't ever knowed it t' fail yet."

Someone began to slap McKay's head from side to side, and he began to sober up rapidly.

"Hey, you," a vaguely familiar voice kept on saying, in between stinging blows. "Hey, you . . . bettin' man, wake up, it's time t' settle yer bet."

Mick McKay split his eyelids to gaze at his lamp-lit tormentors. The Smith boys were all well within striking distance, wearing happy smiles and looking back at him.

"Why you doin' this t' . . . " McKay began, but a swift punch in the mouth burst his lips, broke some teeth and knocked him back painfully hard against a wooden partition. On the other side of the partition startled horses kicked and snorted. Focusing tear-brimmed eyes he rolled on the compacted horse manure and dirt floor, recognizing the place as a livery stable.

Raw fear quickly took the place of the alcohol as cruel hands dragged him back on to his feet. Abe's still-grinning features floated into view.

"Recall that skinny young fella you an' the others strung up . . . the one ya said ya laughed at, because he pissed himself?" Jude growled. His hand gripped both sides of the captive's bleeding mouth. Then he squeezed his thumb and fingers together, so fiercely that they almost caused the inside of McKay's cheeks to meet. "Well, do ya or don't ya?"

Staring wide-eyed with fright and pain, McKay could barely nod.

"Good. Hank Smith was his name." Still maintaining the pressure, he forced McKay to look at each brother in turn. "That's Abe Smith . . . that's Adam Smith." He turned the petrified man back to face him. "And me, I'm Jude Smith . . . we're his kin and we're out t' get even."

Expertly, Abe slung a lasso over one of the beams. Adam caught the end and slipped the noose around McKay's neck then pulled it, dragging the condemned man like a dog on a lead.

The slack was taken up on the rope.

"You like the idea of gettin' ya neck stretched, fella?" Jude asked quietly. Mick, who was shamelessly weeping by this time, shook his head. "All right, now I ain't ever seen a growed man piss his pants, so . . . " — he pointed to McKay's crotch — "go on . . . piss!"

After only a slight pause, the three brothers began to laugh. Jude called out a slow count of three, then they all hauled on the rope with unconcealed pleasure.

Kicking frantically, and with his eyes bulging, the ex-shopkeeper's feet were lifted clear of the straw-strewn ground. The rope was securely tied to a cleat on a roof-support and McKay was left swinging, to choke and to drip dry.

"That's one of 'em dead an' gone," Jude said coldly. "But the fella I'm settin' my sights on, is that smart-arse with the big gun. Oh, yeah . . . I'm gonna get Matt Malone."

7

ANGERED by the seemingly complete lack of action by the law, Malone and the major marched into the town sheriffs office and went to stand directly in front of the lawman.

"Listen, Sheriff, it's more than a g'damned week and a half, since Mick McKay was murdered in this dangblasted one-horse town." He brought the flat of his hand down loudly on the cluttered top of the desk. "And it's not good enough. The God-fearin' folks who've struggled all this way with me on their wagons, they want somethin' done, Sheriff . . . and so do I . . . and soon."

Unperturbed, the sheriff lolled back in his chair and, without looking up, carried on rolling a cigarette.

"Soon, eh?" he drawled, carefully

forming the tube then smoothing it between his fingers. "Soon ain't no time at all." The tip of his tongue delicately licked the edge of the paper, then he stuck it down before slipping the cigarette in between his lips. "The murder of the McKay fella, it's small beer. It ain't a new happenin' around here," the town sheriff admitted.

"Small beer?" The major sounded incredulous.

A match flared and the sheriff lit his smoke, inhaling deeply before continuing. "Sure. It ain't no big deal. This is a mining town. It's rough here. Plenty of drunks get strung up, 'specially on Saturday nights. Scores keep on gettin' settled all the time."

"Then why don't ya get up off your big fatt butt, and do somethin' about it?" Malone growled.

The lawman sighed audibly as he exhaled a steady plume of smoke. The deadpan expression on his rugged face never altered, but his stringy-veined hand slowly swept across his chest until a broken, nicotine-stained fingernail tapped at his tin star.

"See that? It's the only law badge inside a hundred miles of this office." His finger stopped tapping then pointed straight at the centre of his chest, as his chair scraped back noisily. "And there's only me willin' and fool enough to wear it. I can be sick an' dyin' on my feet, but it don't matter a damn to anyone. My responsibilities in this job last all the way around the clock, and every lousy day of the year. With no deputies, no volunteers to help me . . . nothin', except for an occasional posse when folks get hot enough under the collars to act."

Malone and the major exchanged glances. The sheriff watched them, clearly amused but unworried by their awkward silence.

"On your lonesome, eh? That's a horse of a different colour," Matt pointed out at last. "That's too bad. Maybe you've got a point."

"Hmmm." The major noisily cleared

his throat, grimaced and smoothed his side-whiskers before leaning forward to rest both hands on the desk.

"Perhaps some of us from the wagon train can help out while we're here," the major suggested.

Grim-lipped, the sheriff stared at them as though considering the offer, but shook his head.

"Thanks, but no. The town mayor, he'll never agree t' me swearin' extras in. No matter what the job needs. Nope, he's always made it a point that the town can't afford t' pay anyone else."

"You've got it all wrong," the major explained. "It ain't money we want, Sheriff. It's good old-fashioned justice for one of our friends. That's what we're after."

"And quick as ya like," Malone butted in. "To give our folks peace of mind."

The sheriff laughed.

"Quick?"

"Yeah, give the major an' me, and

a couple of the other men, deputy's badges," Matt offered. "Make us official and we'll start askin' around."

"You'll be wastin' yer time, and you'll get the same answers as me. I've already asked. Nobody knows anythin', at least nothin' they'll talk about."

"Give us a try," Matt said. "What ya got to lose, eh?"

The lawman drew hard on his cigarette. It burned down swiftly towards his lips as he pondered on the unusual suggestion. Suddenly he blew out the tobacco smoke in a blue-grey acrid cloud which swirled about him, stinging his eyes and causing him to squint. He nodded.

"All right," he agreed, reaching for the sweat-stained hat hanging on the peg by the office door. "Let's go an' see the mayor." With that he crammed the hat on his head and opened the door. "Come on fellas, nobody can do a dang thing in this town, not without his say-so."

To his surprise, Matt found himself

and the major entering the snugly-carpeted and furnished mayor's parlour. However, it was not the normal type of mayor's parlour he would have expected to find in a house or maybe a town hall. This parlour was located behind the noisy smoke-filled bar room of the Silver Moon saloon, and Mr Mayor wore a fancy gunbelt with a tied-down holster.

"This is Mayor Smith," the lawman informed them after he had given their names to the man slouched in the swivel chair behind the desk. Without the hesitation of shyness, the mayor got to his feet and came towards them, smiling like a hungry alligator. With his hand outstretched, he warmly greeted each in turn.

"Major . . . Malone . . . pleased to know ya, men." With a hard glint in his eye, he added, "I don't care much for all this Mister Mayor stuff. Call me Jude."

★ ★ ★

"Well, I don't like him. There's somethin' about that fella which don't sit right." Matt rubbed his chin. "No, in my estimation, he's about as genuine as a three-legged snake. I could never trust him, Major," he exclaimed as the two of them rode back to where the wagons were camped for the winter. "Oh he seems friendly enough, but there's somethin' that don't fit somehow. It made my skin crawl when I heard the way he talked, like he was God Almighty and one of the boys at the same time."

"Mmm, I've got to admit he didn't impress me any, either," the major replied. "But still, at least we've got things moving at last."

"Uh-huh," Matt said sarcastically. "Even if it's us who've got to do all the movin'."

Drawing closer to the camp they noticed a crowd had gathered in front of one of the wagons. They could hear the raised voices of both men and women in heated argument.

"What in tarnation . . . ?" the major began. Immediately they kicked their mounts into a gallop and headed directly for the trouble-spot.

"Here's Malone an' the major," someone in the crowd cried out. "They'll sort you miners out, good an' quick."

As the horses thundered in to camp then skidded to a stop, the strangers turned to face Matt and the major. Rough men, tough men, stood with their brawny arms akimbo and fierce determination written all over their faces.

"It's the Franklin wagon," Matt called out as they swung down from their saddles.

"I can see that," the major answered tersely. "I didn't retire from the army because I was blind."

His military training in *aid to the civil powers*, came to the fore. Decisively, not bothering to tie up his horse he released the reins, then stepped directly up to the rowdiest, most demonstrative stranger in sight. The man was the most apparent ringleader and therefore the one the major had to control first.

"Well, lookee what we got here," one of the miners jeered. "Seems t' me like somebody's already done gone an' sent for a preacher-man."

The major ignored the fool, concentrating his full authority upon the ringleader.

"Now, then . . . what do you think you men are doin', causing all this shenanigan?"

"Drop dead, Gran'pa," the miner sneered. "Go read yer Bible an' chaw on yer bread an' milk."

"Mind yer mouth, fella," Malone warned, pushing in between the major and the lout.

"Or else what?" the bully smirked.

Smack! The miner said no more. Matt's iron-hard balled fist had smashed into the belligerent man's mouth, splitting his lips and sending him reeling backwards into the arms of his amazed cronies.

In a wave, the miners surged forward with a spontaneous roar, but the sharp crack of a shot rent the air as the major fired his pistol at the sky.

"Stand still. Stay right where you are. The next one of you mining boys . . . or anyone else, who even thinks of stepping out of line, gets himself ventilated." The major swept his intense gaze over the angry faces. The hand holding the still-smoking .45 waved at them. "With this. Savvy?"

"Hey, you the new sheriff?" a miner asked, having spotted the tin star peeking out from the major's vest under his jacket. "The other guy stopped a bullet or somethin', eh?"

"No, he ain't dead," Malone answered. "The major an' me, we're on the law office strength, as volunteer deputies."

"Never mind that," the major snapped, returning to the point. "Why in tarnation are you all here? You on the prod . . . lookin' for trouble?"

136

He picked on a small man. "Why . . . eh?"

"Hell, mister, we don't want no trouble. We heard tell there were widdawomen an' some single gals too, here on these wagons." The diminutive minor doffed his cap, crumpled it between his hands and shifted his feet in his embarrassment. "Ya see, mister, apart from the painted gals in the saloon an' the whorehouse, women are in short supply around here. We're all after gettin' us some proper women . . . ladies, if ya know what ah mean . . . the marryin' kind."

"Wives, eh?" For a while the major stood with his chin in his hand, his shrewd eyes roving over the expectant faces before him. As usual his thumb and finger tugged at his whiskers while he considered the matter.

"Well, did you honestly believe you would simply come on over here and take women away with you?" Before anyone had chance to answer his question, he went on, "Now I'm not saying that none of the ladies would be willing, but . . . I'll tell you what I'll do."

Curious, everyone went quiet, straining their ears, and waiting for the major's words of wisdom.

"You fellas go on back to your shacks at the diggin's, clean and smarten yourselves up, and then, come back here at noon t'morrow. Maybe if the ladies in question see good upstandin' men instead of . . . animals, they'll be tempted to look on you with more kindly eyes."

"And we can take 'em then?" asked an eager voice.

"No it doesn't mean that. However, between now and then, I'll have a serious talk with the ladies who are free to marry and ask what they think on the idea." He held out his hands expressively as he shrugged. "Who knows, a few of you could be lucky. Some of them might find the idea of marriage attractive."

★ ★ ★

The major had been away from the conestoga for some time. Malone was startled when someone rapped with bare knuckles on the tailboard behind him. At the same time a familiar voice called his name.

"Mister Malone? Hello, it's me . . . Mary Franklin. Have you a moment?"

He pulled back the canvas and shivered as the frost-laden air chilled him. Looking down he noted the signs of worry in her features.

"Of course, ya can have as long as ya want." He held out his hand to help her. "Come on up, Mrs Franklin."

"Mary . . . I've told you before, call me Mary, please."

They settled down to sit at opposite sides of the conestoga, each with the inevitable mug of steaming hot coffee clutched in their hands to warm them.

"Major Mortimer's been giving the widows and single women a chat."

Shyly she let her gaze drop to her cup. "No doubt you know what it was about."

"Uh-huh," he agreed, unaware that he sounded bored. He wondered what this preamble was all leading up to.

She waited, expecting him to say more, but when he did not, she continued. This time she spoke quietly and with a faint hint of despair in her words.

"I'd be grateful if you'd give me your advice." Suddenly she put her coffee mug down and wrung her hands. "I have William to consider. A boy needs a man about the house."

"Yep, that seems reasonable. A man can be real handy t' have around a place," Matt agreed.

"Yes, to keep him right." She perked up a bit more. "To advise him about things . . . manly things, those things that a mother can't."

"Manly things?" Malone almost grinned but restrained himself. "You don't have to worry none on that score.

140

Not with your boy. Yes, ma'am, you wait an' see. Willy's growin' up fast. He's gonna make out real fine."

"At the meeting, with the major . . ." Mary Franklin blurted out, "several of the women expressed the opinion that it would be better to stay here with a stranger for a husband, than to risk continuing with the wagon train again when the springtime arrives."

He stared across at her.

"And is that what you believe?" he asked.

"I don't know." She lifted up her mug again and stared into it as though it was a crystal ball. "I miss Gregory . . . my husband. It's not the hardship or even the dangers of the journey. Such things don't bother me. I can easily face up to them without blinking an eye. It's just . . ." She hesitated, and when she looked at him, he noticed tears brimming. "It's so . . . lonely for me, even with my boy."

Malone scratched at his head then

wrinkled his brow as he fingered his cheeks.

"I don't know what to suggest, er . . . "

"Mary," she prompted.

He felt foolish, saying her name. But he did. Apart from the normal single man's use of whores and bar girls, he had always shied away from the marryin'-kind of women.

"Some miners make a real good livin', if they have a lucky streak. To my mind, this ain't much of a town t' look at, or live in, but on the other hand, I guess ya could do worse."

A tear bulged suddenly, then overflowed and zig-zagged down her cheek. Self-consciously she sniffed and dabbed at the wetness with a clean, delicate handkerchief of white lace.

Looking away he tried to steer clear and close the subject.

"Why don't you go back to your wagon and talk it over with Willy?" Pleased with his own suggestion, he smiled. "Yeah, that's it, he's a smart kid. Ask him. See what his ideas are."

"We've talked already." She sat upright as though having arrived at a decision. But she stopped speaking and bit her lip, letting the time tick on by.

"Well," he pressed at last when he could no longer stand the strain. "What's he say?"

Fearful, she began to shake visibly.

"He said . . . he said . . . "

"Yeah . . . what's he say?"

"He thinks . . . " She gazed back into the coffee mug and her knuckles showed shiny white with the force of her grip. "He . . . "

Apprehension was building up inside him. Matt could smell his own sweat and felt it begin to trickle down his neck even though the temperature inside the wagon was not much above freezing. Suddenly, and for no good reason he could think of, he raised his voice and blurted out a question.

"For Christ's sake woman, what's he say?"

Startled, jumping as if he'd drawn his handgun, she began to weep.

"William told me that he definitely doesn't want me to marry a miner . . . or anyone else." She made a valiant effort, pressed her lips together, sniffed and blinked a few times to dispel the tears.

Matt heaved a sigh of relief, resorting to the coffee mug to hide his confusion. Then she opened her mouth ready to speak once more, and he tensed again.

"He told me, and please credit that I speak only the truth." She stopped for a moment as though expecting Malone to confirm this. He did not, so she took another breath and carried on. "William was in deadly earnest, that if I am to marry at all, then the man I accept . . . has got to be you." She gabbled out the latter words at top speed, flushing scarlet and turning away to avoid his pop-eyed gaze of sheer bewilderment.

"What?" Malone let his jaw drop.

Coffee spilled down his chin as he gagged, and coughed, almost choking when his swallow was interrupted. Only after his fit of coughing was over and he was left gasping, did he ask, "Lady . . . did I hear you right?"

"Yes, I'm sure you did," she told him softly. Then she turned back to face him once more. This time she ventured a mischievous smile. "It's your own fault, Mr Malone. You're his real-life hero . . . so you see, no one else will do, will they?"

8

"**T**HE bastard's what?" Abe asked incredulously, not certain if his brother was joking or not.

"It's the gospel truth," Adam stated, fanning his hand of cards again, then taking a second cautious glance at them before tossing a red chip on to the green baize. "He's gettin' himself hitched to one o' them wagon-train females, an English widda woman."

"English eh?" Abe paused to think before he said, "Ya know, once when I was crazy-drunk, way down to Sante Fe, I had me an English gal one night."

"Never heard ya mention that before," Jude drawled, hardly interested.

"Well it was no big shakes." Abe's features twisted in a display of disgust. "If Logan's woman's anythin' like her, it's likely as not her puss's like the rear end of a fat old cow."

The others concentrated on their poker game. In an attempt to regain their attention, and to emphasize his point, Abe spat emphatically into the brass spittoon which stood on the floor next to Jude. Then, using the toe of his boot he hooked out a chair from the table, spun it round and knees open wide, straddled it. Propping his chin on his fist, he rested his elbows on the top rail of the chair-back, rocking the chair on two creaking legs.

"Yeah," he sneered, "bet her back-end matches that too."

"Now that's just where you're wrong, boy. I've seen her. She's a real good-looker. Talks kinda fancy though, and walks about with that head of hers held high, like she owns the place. But I tell ya, I've got t' hand it to Malone," Jude ruefully admitted with a shake of his head. "Ah sure wouldn't kick 'er out of my bedroll on a frosty night. No sir, not even if I had me a broken back."

Adam laughed nervously and took yet another sly peep at his cards before he opened his mouth again.

"Hecky-me, Jude," Adam blurted out, "judgin' from some of the gals I've seen you with, you wouldn't kick a scabby pig out of yer bunk . . . well, not before it was more than a month dead."

"That a fact?" Jude grinned wickedly, picked up a pile of chips and slapped one on top of his brother's last contribution. "Well this's to cover that, and . . . " — he made a point of counting out ten more, slowly; only then did he shove them into the centre of the kitty — "just for fun and t' make ya suffer, I raise ya ten more."

Adam's laughter trailed off then died. Always the careful one, money was a serious business to him. He held his cards close to his chest, fanned them and secretively checked his hand again.

"You're bluffin' . . . ain't ya?" Adam laughed again. The laugh had been forced, and when Jude did not answer, he put on a brave face. "Yeah, I'm sure y' are." The grin lingered, but the deep wrinkles on his brow and the tone of his voice told the others that his confidence was bleeding away.

"Well, my money says big brother's got ya licked," Abe yawned. "Give in. Let him take the pot before you go an' lose everythin' ya got."

"Ya think ah'm smokin' loco weed?" Adam looked from one to the other. "Ya both believe ah'm gonna be fool enough t' sling my hand in . . . and" — he turned back to Jude — "you'll be left sittin' there laughin', with nothin' but maybe a jack high or a pair of deuces." Puffing out his chest, he sat up straight and attempted to look superior. "No way, Jude. You ain't bluffin' me again."

Sitting at the other side of the table, Jude remained relaxed and cool, in every outward way looking his normal smug self. He returned the grin.

"Bluffin'? Yeah, maybe I am . . . but

on the other hand, maybe I'm not. One thing I do know, it'll cost ya to find out." He leaned forward. "The English woman . . . the one Malone's gettin hitched to, she used t' belong to that doctor fella."

"Doctor?" Abe frowned. "What doctor?"

"You know. The doc . . . that guy on the wagon train, the fella young Hank blasted." Jude kept his voice matter of fact, without allowing his gaze to stray from Adam, who with a fresh maggot of doubt gnawing at him, was reconsidering his cards. "He was the fella the young fool went an' got himself strung up for."

"Will you two old women put yer knittin' down an' quit your jawin'?" Adam growled as the raw edges of his nerves began to show. "Can't ya give a fella an even break? Let me concentrate, will ya?"

"What ya gonna do about it . . . this weddin'?" Abe asked. "Ya gonna spoil things for Malone?"

"You bet . . . but not 'til I'm good an' ready like I told ya before. Once he gets himself hitched, I'll be able t' put the pressure on . . . make 'im suffer all the more. You'll see. I'm plannin' to make his pain last a long time." He leered, nodded once, slowly, and winked. "And another thing. I'm gonna try out his woman, real good." Leaning back in his chair he returned his full attention to Adam. "But first I'm gonna have the shirt off this gamblin' man's back."

"Oh no. Ya ain't that lucky." Adam tossed caution to the wind. "You're bluffin'. I can tell by yer eyes, so I'm callin' ya." Throwing his chips nonchalantly on to the table, he sniggered. "Come on, smart-arse . . . show me what yer made of. What ya got?"

Jude heaved a heavy sigh, the smile no longer on his lips. Slowly he spread his cards face up along the table then stared into the pallid face opposite him.

"Too much for you, boy." He grinned wickedly. "A pride o' kings, and they're ridin' a pair of ladies."

Adam kicked his chair back and stood up. With his teeth clenched, he raised his hand high above his head before slamming his cards on to the table.

"G'damn ya, I had me a pair of aces backed by a pair o' deuces." Angrily he snatched his cards up then slammed them back down again, this time with even more force. "G'damn, I swear, you've the devil sittin' on yer shoulder every time I play ya."

"But two pair, they don't beat a full house, Adam. Not no how." Abe chuckled, slapping his losing brother playfully on the back. "Ya'll never learn . . . ya should've knowed better than to try to bluff it out with him. Hell, boy, there ain't nobody like Jude . . . he always wins a bluff."

★ ★ ★

"Told ya you'd get nowhere with McKay's murder," the sheriff pointed out as Malone and the major were about to leave the law office. "Murders are like that. If ya don't get 'em sorted and settled straight away, they drag on forever."

"I thought we'd have nailed the killer by now," the major sighed. "I'm disappointed, I feel like we've let the little fella down. I was sure we were on to somethin' when all those witnesses saw him inside the Silver Moon."

"Yeah," Matt grimaced. "The mayor an' everybody saw him, right until he went back out through the doorway . . . on his ownsome." Pulling up his coat collar ready to go out into the driving snow, he said, "After he left the saloon, no one admits t' seein' him alive. It's a real pity. I'd like to meet up with whoever did that to the poor guy."

"Forget it," the sheriff advised. "If I was in your boots I'd be thinkin' about your comin' weddin'."

"Don't say that to the fella," the major grinned. "He's been tryin' to keep his mind off that and not doing a very good job, either."

A flurry of snowflakes swirled around them as they stepped out into the darkness, banging the door behind them.

"Jesus, don't it ever stop snowin' around these parts?" Malone gasped as the crisp cold air chilled his face. "I was frozen to the bone tryin' t' sleep in the sack last night."

"Wait 'til you're wed . . . there ain't a thing invented that'll warm you like a good woman. And you've landed one of the best. You don't know how lucky you are."

"Lucky?" Matt clutched his coat collar closer to his throat and, head down, the two of them trudged through the knee-deep snow, heading for the camp. "Guess I am. Ya know, it seems impossible. I can't believe what I've done . . . sayin' yes to her proposal. Even after a couple of months, I can't be sure I ain't dreamin' it all up."

The wagon master chuckled, resting his hand on Matt's shoulder as they strolled between the ranks of wagons. He offered some advice.

"Well, son, you'd better believe it. You've given the woman your word on it. And how about the town mayor, offering you the main bar of the Silver Moon for your weddin'? He didn't have to do that you know. I tell you, everyone on the train's looking forward to the shindig. Whatever else you do, don't even consider tryin' to back out now . . . not unless you want to find out what it's like to get lynched."

"Maybe bein' hung'll be less painful than gettin' married," Malone reasoned. "I ain't never been tied down before."

* * *

The waiting was over. The winter had dragged to an end and with the spring thaw came the wedding day. Everything went like clockwork. Before he knew it, Matt, no longer a bachelor, now possessed a ten-year-old stepson as well as a fine wife.

Like everyone else from the wagon train, they were enjoying the party food, along with the cheerful foot-stamping music of a fiddle and the jangling saloon piano.

"Well, Mr Malone," his new bride said in his ear as Matt whirled and guided her among the other dancers. "How does it feel to be four hours married and dancing a polka with your wife?"

"Fine . . . better than I thought it would be." He winked then grinned broadly at her. "Yeah, this marriage seems t' be lastin' out all right. Who knows, maybe with a little luck, I could get used to it."

"Good." She flashed him a smile. "I'd hate William to be disappointed. After all, you did promise you'd teach him to hunt."

Suddenly she stiffened and craned her neck towards the swing doors of the saloon. Matt's own attention naturally followed suit.

A drunken miner, judging by his clothes, had entered the saloon. He stood there, bleary-eyed and swaying stupidly as he tried to focus on the dancers. As no one challenged his reason for being there, the drunk staggered on, directly for the dance floor. Then the boy was there, bravely attempting to stop the man in his tracks.

"I'd better go and take a look-see," Matt explained. Disengaging himself from Mary he strode across the floor. He was just in time to see the miner grip William's shirt-front and lift him off his feet.

"What ya mean, private?" the drunk yelled aggressively above the sound of the music. "It's a friggin' saloon, sonny-boy."

"Put the kid down, fella." Malone's words brimmed with menace and the miner paused for a second. Then with a roar of rage he hurled the boy at Matt, who deftly caught the lad, cushioning his landing.

"Stay back, Willy," Malone told him curtly, pushing him aside with more force than he liked to use on the boy. "You keep well back an' out of my way, I've got me a job t' do."

The music had trailed off to a discordant and impromptu halt. The couples stopped dancing and rubbernecked to see what was going on beside the doorway.

Suddenly, women cried out in alarm as the burly drunk whipped out a broad-bladed knife from its sheath, tied to his leg, a little way above his knee. Crouching low, spider-like he sidled closer, his eyes fixed on Malone as he kept on tossing his knife from hand to hand in an attempt to confuse his quarry. All at once he seemed deadly sober.

"Come on pretty boy," he taunted Matt, waving him closer with his hand. "Come an' try your luck." His yellowed, brown-stained teeth were bared in a vicious snarl and saliva dripped onto his chin.

"Now look here, mister," began Malone, "this is my weddin' day. Everybody's happy and I ain't in no mood for fightin' you or anyone else, so why don't ya put that thing back in its sheath." He smiled and held out his hand in friendship, adding, "Come on, I'll buy ya a drink before you go."

"Don't need no friggin' drink from you, mister."

"There's ladies present, so watch yer mouth, fella," Malone warned.

"Oh yeah? Well, you watch this!" The miner lunged forward, slashing and stabbing with amazing speed. A woman screamed. Blood gushed as the knife penetrated Matt's open palm, the point emerging from the back of his hand as he defended himself.

The knifeman twisted the blade, jerked it free of the flesh and held it ready to strike again.

Then a pistol fired, sounding louder than normal in the enclosed space, and a widening blue smoke-ring hovered, twisting in the air as the drunk slammed back on to a table beside the doors. The table tilted slowly, overbalanced and went over, taking the corpse to the floor with a thud.

A shocked silence followed, and the stillness, coupled with the stench of burned powder, told everyone that the fight was over.

"Oh sweet Jesus," Malone gasped out, clenching his teeth. He felt his knees grow weak, as those closest rushed to help him.

Almost as quickly, the deceptively alert bartender vaulted over the bar. Pushing through the throng he used a clean towel to bandage the injured hand and staunch the flow of blood.

Through the haze of pain, Matt became aware that his new wife and boy were beside him, quietly concerned and offering gentle comfort. A couple of feet behind them, the town mayor stood unperturbed, calmly replacing the spent shell. He holstered his gun as Malone caught his eye.

"Thanks . . . for what ya did just then," Matt called out. "I guess I owe ya one."

A strange smile spread over Jude Smith's face. His lips twisted and his eyes sparkled with a hint of amusement. Before turning away, he nodded.

"Yeah. That you do, Malone . . . that you do."

★ ★ ★

Later that same evening, in the hotel room the major had booked for the honeymoon night, after the operation on Malone's hand, the doc quietly snapped shut the catches of his medical bag.

"Doctor, my husband's hand," Mary Malone whispered, "it looks a dreadful mess."

"I'll not argue with your observation," the fort saw-bones whispered back. "In fact, I'd say that's pretty accurate."

"Please, Doctor." She pursed her

161

lips. "Don't treat me like a child, I used to be a doctor's wife, so tell me the truth. Will his hand heal properly, or won't it?"

The medic shrugged as he hefted the bag.

"Heal? Yes ma'am, barrin' any accidents it'll heal all right. Your husband's a fit man." With his free hand he rubbed at his jaw, considering his answer. "As to, 'properly' . . . well, I ain't God Almighty, but with an educated guess, I'd say he'll never make a livin' playin' the piano. Maybe, if he's real lucky, and I do mean real lucky, he'll be able to move a finger or two on that hand. But not much more."

Grasping at straws, trying to do her best for her man, Mary Malone pressed the army surgeon further.

"But supposing I took him back east?" There was worry but no panic in her words. "I do have money available. Maybe if I take him to see a specialist?"

Her talking trailed off when she

saw him shaking his head and smiling sadly.

"It ain't the money, Mrs Malone. You'd be wastin' your time. It wouldn't help none, not even if you took him along t'see the Holy Ghost. It was a mighty big blade that stabbed him. It looks to me like it went in straight, then twisted and dragged on the way out. That way it did a lot of damage to tendons an' things."

He trod quietly towards the hotel-room door and opened it. "I'm sorry, ma'am, but I thought it wise to relieve his pain. I've given him somethin'."

"Of course," she said softly. "Thank you, I'm grateful and quite understand."

He pressed his lips together hard, showing his doubt as she followed close behind.

"I'm not so certain that you do understand." Once again his shoulders peaked into a shrug. "Oh, and another thing. Sorry, but that medicine I got down him, it's gonna make him sleep. It'll be a real, deep sleep, if you catch my drift. So ya see, I guess this ain't gonna be what you'd call, a spectacular honeymoon."

From life-long habit, he stood to attention, clicked his heels and executed a military salute. Then he smiled again.

"By the way, dear lady, I never had the opportunity to say it to you before, but . . . congratulations!"

9

TO the surviving members of the wagon train who had endured the almost non-stop misery of the winter camp, the spectacle of the government men moving out from the fort, cheered them. To protect the technical equipment and baggage train which trundled along in their wake, the cavalry troops rode two abreast.

After a winter confined mainly to humdrum duties such as weapons maintenance, cleaning and the like, the troopers' uniforms, sabres and harness gleamed like new. The horses, sensing the promise of new grass, pranced and bounced on their toes. To the watchers it was a welcome sight which assured everyone that spring had really arrived.

It was obvious to all that if an army troop, hampered by heavily loaded

wagons, could travel over the ground
. . . so could the conestogas.

A wildfire of excitement rippled through the camp like a contagious disease, infecting everybody with the urge to be on the move and get back on the trail for Oregon. The place buzzed like a beehive. Women set to, cleaning the conestogas. They did extra scrubbing at their washboards, knowing they would have little opportunity to clean bedding and such when on the road.

Men checked and rechecked the workings of the wagons, greased axles and replaced brake blocks, cleaned all of their firearms, cast bullets and sharpened axes.

Teams of horses seemed to be continually queuing outside the livery forge, waiting to be re-shod and have spares made. The town blacksmith, lathered in sweat, swore and cursed, but worked on, glad of the business bonanza brought to him. As he worked, small children watched from the safety of the stockyard fence, listening with delight and undisguised awe at his extensive vocabulary of epithets.

At the wagon camp, older boys were set to work, saddle-soaping each and every harness until the leather returned to its proper suppleness and shone once again like well-polished boots.

Victuals and general stores were replenished from the mercantile in town, along with ammunition and what medicines were available.

Then, taking almost everyone by surprise, the wagon train was ready. The drivers sat with the reins in their hands, tense and waiting for the off. Then the major yelled the order. Whips cracked, drivers shouted encouragement to their teams, and children cheered. The wagon train started to creak and roll, heading north again, to rejoin the original route westward.

"Well, it's about time. Oregon, here we come," the major beamed as he rode alongside Malone's wagon. "Sometimes

I doubted we'd ever leave this town. But here we are, the beginnin' of the last leg. We've left the worst behind us, in them there mountains yonder."

"Maybe. Hope so." Matt did not feel too sure, although he himself was glad to be on the move. "But I wouldn't care t' bet on that. We'll be passin' through snake country for quite a way. An' the snakes don't take kindly t' others crossin' on their land. Especially us white folks."

"Snakes?" his newly acquired son asked from his seat next to Matt. "What sort of snakes?"

"The Indian sort. Shoshoni snakes, that's the handle they go by, on account of the northern part o' that tribe livin' around Snake river."

"Are they dangerous?" the boy asked, thrilled by the idea.

"Only when they try t' kill ya," Matt grinned at the boy.

"I don't believe the Shoshoni will bother us," the major predicted confidently. "Not in springtime. Not when there'll be plenty of game around for everyone."

"You've a fair point there, Major," Matt agreed. "A full belly tends to keep everyone happy."

"How's the hand, Matt? Can you move your fingers any better?"

"Well, nothin's dropped off yet, so I reckon it must be on the mend. Don't hurt much anyhow." Malone held his right hand out for the major to see. "Not a pretty sight but there's some movement in my thumb and first two fingers." He twitched the fingers to demonstrate. "Unless I learn t' draw and shoot with my left hand, I may as well give my gunbelt and revolver to young Willy, here."

Willy gasped.

"You mean it . . . really?" As Malone gave an expressive shrug, the boy almost exploded with excitement. "Wow! I'll be able to fight those snakes if they come to attack us."

"Get out of that one, Malone," the major said out of the side of his mouth.

Then, grinning over his shoulder as he cantered away towards that days lead wagon, he called back. "Bet you ain't goin' to be very popular with his momma."

* * *

"When we gonna go after 'em?" Abe asked as the three Smith brothers looked out through an upstairs window of the Silver Moon, from where they could watch the line of wagons trundling into the distance. "In another hour they'll be out of sight over the horizon."

"Yeah, and that much closer to the army boys who rode out ahead of 'em," Jude reminded him. "Ya wanna fight it out with the army?" He raised his eyebrows to a peak. "Ya want Adam an' me to commit suicide with ya?"

"We've waited all winter, so they'll keep a bit longer, won't they?" Adam put in. "Besides, we don't want our tame sheriff gettin' any wrong ideas

170

about us respectable Smith boys, do we?"

"That's right, we'll give 'em a day or two before we let the folks around here know that we're goin' on a . . . business trip." The mayor moved away from the window. "The last time I spoke to the army commander, he told me that the army's first job is to go back through the pass, then along the mountain trail and clear that avalanche damage. That's on account of it havin' to be ready for the next settlers to come on through the pass. So you know what that means, don't ya?"

"No, what?" Abe frowned, hooding his eyes. "I don't get ya."

Adam struck his forehead with the palm of his hand.

"Mule-head! If the army's gonna be . . . " — he pointed dramatically to his left — "east, by the time we set out after the wagon train, who'll be headin' . . . " — this time he pointed to his right — "west! The soldier boys'll be miles away. We'll be safe t' do any

171

damn thing we want, won't we?"

"We'll take a few extra bottles of fire-water and baccy twists along to our breed friend," Jude cut in. "An' ya know what he'll do for that stuff, don't ya? Yeah, we'll be able to sit back and wait for the plums t' drop in our laps."

"Yeah," Abe's eyes lit up. "Then we'll take our time, squeezin' the pips out of Malone an' the rest of them bastards."

"Talkin' of Malone," Adam said. "Ya think, when it's healed, that hacked-up hand of his'll let him use a gun?"

"No way," Abe came back. "That bum miner we hired t' cut him up made a good job of that." He laughed. "Jesus, I thought he was gonna slice the whole damned paw off his arm." Grinning wider he went on to ask, "Did ya see the look on the dumb fool miner's face when Jude drew on him and blasted him away?"

"Made me a lot of friends there, didn't I?" Jude smirked. "The Malones and everyone else on the wagon train became my pal after that." Holding his jacket lapels as a politician would when making a speech, he declared, "And that . . . little brothers, was what could be called a real good move. A smart move. In fact, any business man worth his salt would describe it as a solid investment for the future."

* * *

Having rejoined the Oregon trail, the travellers discovered the ground to be swampy in many places due to the extra quick thaw. The wheels of the wagons bogged down, sometimes axle-deep or more, causing hours of extra backbreaking work for man and beast alike.

To try and avoid this disruption of their time-planned programme, Malone resumed his original scouting job. He would ride ahead, check the trouble-spots then find detours which, although further to travel, saved a lot of time and much physical effort.

Each morning, Matt would use a hand axe to cut himself a bundle of willow wands. Then he would strip the bark off to make them visible, and stick these in the ground as markers for the lead wagon to follow during detours.

Keen to get away from the monotonously slow pace of the wagons, William gladly rode out early each day alongside his stepfather to help. His task consisted of dismounting and sticking the slender wands vertically into the earth where Matt told him to.

Malone did not go out of his way to hunt game for the pot. There was no point in doing so. The travellers still had full larders and were using the fresh supplies bought before they left the mining town. Because of this Matt had more time to scout further ahead and prepare the trail.

"This'll do for tonight's camp-site. Shove three sticks in together, to let 'em know that," he explained to William. "We'll move on a while, stake out another three or four miles to give us a good start t'morrow, then well get back an' see what yer momma's fixed us for supper."

* * *

Two pairs of keen eyes watched Malone and the boy until they had ridden out of sight beyond the rise.

"That's one o' the bastards I'm after, Little Bear," Jude pointed out to the half-breed. "And it's his woman I aim to have."

Little Bear said nothing, only nodded and drew his dirty finger across his own throat.

"Oh, that fella's in for a heap worse than a slit throat," Jude grinned. "I want him t' to be a long time in dyin' . . . a real long time."

The half-breed nodded his agreement. Then he gave an evil smile.

"Me have boy?"

"Yeah," Jude told him. "Why not? Do what ya like with him. He ain't no use t' me, or the boys."

Pointing, then jerking his head in the direction Matt and the boy had taken, Little Bear made as if to go after them.

"No, not now, ya damned fool," Jude snapped out angrily. "I've told ya, I want his woman first. As soon as I've got her, that's when your brother's tribe moves in t' wipe out the wagon train."

"Whiskey!" Little Bear stated gruffly, holding out his hand. "You give . . . now."

Jude shook his head and forced a passage through the flexible branches. "No. When I have the woman . . . you get the whiskey." Ignoring the half-breed Shoshoni's petulant facial display of disappointment, he walked out from the elder bushes. Withdrawing the three hazel-wand markers from the ground, he handed them to Little Bear. "Here, you know what t' do with these. Better get movin', we've not much time."

Back-tracking, they pulled out each of the de-barked willow wands until, at a previously selected place, Little Bear began to lay another trail with them. This time, in an entirely different direction.

"Right, Little Bear," Jude said as he prepared to ride away, leaving the half-breed. "Ya know what t' do, but be sure an' wait 'til me an' the woman's well clear of the wagons before you fellas whoop it up." He pulled up his mount as an afterthought struck him. "And Little Bear, just you remember . . . if ya see that fella I showed ya with the kid. I want him alive." He made a drinking motion with his hand. "Extra whiskey if ya fetch him to me."

The breed spread five fingers, and held them up.

"That many bottles."

Jude pondered for a moment.

"Yeah, all right, five . . . but only if he's trussed up and unharmed."

★ ★ ★

177

Mary Malone was taking a break from sitting cramped on the bone-shaking driving seat of the conestoga. Instead, she stretched her legs by walking alongside the wagon, with the reins bunched in her hands. From time to time she flicked the leathers along the swaying backs of the team keeping them at an easy walking pace.

As luck would have it, her rig was next to the last in line on that particular day. The train was negotiating a winding section of the trail between lightly wooded banks. From time to time the wagon ahead disappeared from view as it went round each bend. And for the same reason, she herself went out of sight of the wagon driver coming along behind.

There was a rustle of branches behind her and before she could turn to see the reason for the noise, a leather-gloved hand was clamped over her mouth, preventing any outcry she might give. A sharp jabbing pain in her ribs told her that a pistol threatened her life.

She could smell rancid male sweat, and tobacco on the man's breath as his head pressed close behind hers.

"Don't make a squeak, Mrs Malone. Come quietly and yer son might keep his balls."

Mary Malone twisted her head and stared with wide-eyed horror at the man who had saved her husband's life from the knifeman. She attempted to speak but the hand clamped harder, bruising her lips against her teeth.

He shook his head as a warning, then, pulled the reins from her grasp, flinging them to the ground before he dragged her off the trail and into the bushes. Behind her she heard the team plodding on, monotonously following the trail of the others up ahead as they had done every day since they had started out.

When the last wagon rumbled past then went out of earshot, Jude spoke again.

"Keep rememberin' what I said about yer son. I don't want to hear a single word from them pretty little lips o' yours 'til I say so. Right?" As she made no signal he jerked her head around and glared at her. "Right?"

She nodded. It would be pointless screaming.

"Mighty sensible of ya," he declared, pushing her roughly through the undergrowth until they emerged into a sunlit small clearing. Here, the other brothers sat their horses, grinning and leering down at her.

"Well I do declare," Adam sniggered. "That's one marriage that don't look like it's gonna last too long."

"Where's my son . . . and my husband?" she demanded as soon as the hand left her mouth.

That same hand swung back, its force rattling her teeth as it slapped her cheek. She reeled and staggered like a drunk, fighting hard to stay on her feet.

"Told ya to shut yer mouth, didn't I, woman?" Jude snarled. "Now do as yer told, get up on that horse before I throw yer head down across it like a side o' bacon . . . and," he threatened, "keep yer mouth shut!"

Mary felt tears spill down her cheeks and could taste the salt of her own blood from her split lip as she sat astride the wide-bodied gelding. Her clothing, unsuitable for riding, was rucked up, but before she could adjust it, her hands were grasped and bound tightly to the horn of the saddle. A draught of cool wind blew on to her bare skin, telling her that her underclothes were clearly visible to the lecherous ogling of the younger Smiths.

"Hey, Jude," Abe called, pointing at the patch of white skin, "if yer sellin' any of that, ya can take my order right now."

"And you shut yer fool mouth, same as her," Jude warned, kicking his horse into an uncomfortable trot, and dragging her mount alongside his own. "Ya know me, I don't ever share my women with anyone . . . not even their husbands."

10

THE wagon train closed up like a concertina from front to rear and came to a confused halt. Major Mortimer, cursing angrily, dug in his heels and galloped up to the lead wagon to find out the reason for the stoppage. On arrival, the cause was glaringly easy to see.

Leaping from his horse, as easily as men half his age, he strode over to stand alongside the left-hand rear wheel of the lead wagon, the only wheel not yet submerged. He could go no further himself without sinking into glutinous mud and green, slimy algae.

Already the helpless team were belly-deep in the swamp and the conestoga was well on its way to the same fate. The driver's wife and children were screaming, crying fit to drive a man mad, while the panic-stricken animals rolled the whites of their eyes as they lurched and thrashed, attempting to escape.

To crown it all, the trail was a dead-end. The whole wagon train was trapped in a low-walled box canyon, not as wide as the average wagon and team combined.

"What in blazin' hell-fire has Malone been thinkin' of?" the wagon master ranted to no one in particular. "He tryin' to wreck my reputation along with this whole damned train?"

Then his military training came to the fore and he sprang into confident action, spouting out orders left and right.

"Unhitch the teams of the next three wagons, bring 'em here and hook 'em on, pronto. Fetch ropes. You, you and you, chop branches and shove 'em under the wheels. Pile some brushwood in front of the wagon so the horses can get a footing when we heave 'em out." He waved his arms, urging them to speed up. "Come on, you men, you ain't on vacation . . . get the damned lead out!"

"Major? Major Mortimer, sir," panted a voice from behind. "I think somethin's wrong."

"You're tellin' me, somethin's wrong," the major said, rolling his eyes skyward in his despair. "I'll say it is."

"No sir, you don't understand. I'm drivin' the last wagon in the line. But I can't go on."

The major peered at the sweating man as he gasped and panted, struggling to regain his breath.

"Mister Jones . . . nobody can go on." Pointing an arm past the stricken wagon, he said, "See? We, are in a box canyon."

"No, Major. You don't understand. It's Mrs Malone . . . she's not there. Her wagon's blocking the road." Jones looked as if he would break down and weep. Helplessly he flapped his arms against his sides. "The wagon. The horses. The whole caboodle, it's just standin' there. We've tried, but we can't get round it, no how."

The major wrinkled his brow and, calming down, leaned closer then spoke softly.

"What d'you mean . . . Mrs Malone's gone?"

"Just what I said Major. She ain't there. At first the wife an me, we just pulled up behind her rig. Thought she'd been caught short by a call of nature. You know how it is with womenfolk. So we waited. After about ten minutes or so, and when she didn't turn up, I got my shot-gun, just in case there'd been a bear or somethin', then went to look for her. Tried lookin' both sides of the trail. She's not there, Major . . . believe me, honest t' God she's not."

"Oh, I believe you, Mr Jones. Thanks for tellin' me." The major stroked his side whiskers. There was more trouble on the way. Bad trouble. He could feel it in the air, heavy and brooding as if before a summer thunderstorm. Making up his mind, he shouted to those around him.

"Those workin' the teams to drag this one out, carry on doin' that, but be quick. All the others, get back to your own rigs and arm yourselves. Get ready. I think we're goin' to be attacked at any moment." He shooed them away with his arms as though chasing away chickens. "Go on, scat. Keep your eyes peeled. Watch out for bushwhackers, and see you tell everyone else in the line."

Heaving and sweating, the men allocated to retrieve the bogged-down wagon slowly began to show results. The extra teams hauling on the chains and ropes, snorted and strained. Gradually, dragging the rig an inch at a time, they pulled it free of the mire.

As soon as the mud-caked wagon stood on firm ground, its owner unhitched the team while the conestoga was heaved well clear, allowing more room to work at the task of saving the exhausted animals. The chains and ropes were transferred to the floundering team. Then the owner gave the signal to pull.

At that precise moment, something unseen swished through the air and he fell sideways to splosh face down. Slowly, traces of his final breath bubbled up through the thick green slime. High up in his back a Shoshoni war arrow showed why he lay there. His wife started to scream, and her kids joined in again.

"Indians!" The cry went up, jangling nerves as the call was repeated many times, sending the information in relays along the line of wagons like air bubbles in a water pipe. The sinking horses were left to their now inevitable fate as everyone took cover and scanned along the lip of the narrow canyon for more signs of the ambushers.

It was no more than five minutes before the next attack, but to those waiting, it felt like five hours. This time there was more than a single arrow. Braves had infiltrated through the trees and bushes at the opening of the canyon, and now moved stealthily along on either side of the wagon trail, preparing for their main attack.

The first the travellers knew of this sortie was when the terrified scream of the woman in the last wagon was cut short. Two shot-gun blasts were followed by shots from a pistol. After that, came another long creepy silence.

The Shoshoni slunk along like ghosts, unseen and deadly. With axes and knives, they killed and scalped everyone in the last four wagons. Only when the war party no longer had the advantage of greenery to hide them, did the defenders have a chance to get on level terms.

Guns of all calibres and types were fired at random into the warriors in the narrow gaps on either side of the train. This concentrated fire from men, women and the older children had its desired effect, driving the Shoshoni back under cover.

Shortly after that, arrows and rocks began to rain down from the lip of the canyon above. The arrows posed little danger to people under cover. But the rocks were a different matter. When they happened to strike a wagon, they ripped through canvas sheeting, smashed through bottomboards, shattered wheels, demolished family treasures, crushed living flesh . . . and killed.

"Everyone out of the wagons," ordered the major, moving about fearlessly in the open. "Go to opposite sides of the canyon. Keep close to the cliffs then direct your fire at those varmints up on the ridge facing you."

As people hesitated, the wagon master repeated his instructions twice more before getting the desired results. But by this simple action, they were able to see their targets more easily.

In their turn, the attacking Shoshoni were forced to lean further out over the side of the canyon, exposing themselves.

Bullets struck home. The first few braves tumbled off the edge. Now the hail of projectiles from above was dramatically reduced and more haphazard.

* * *

"Someone's firing, back there. Behind those trees I think," William remarked, twisting in his saddle and pointing to where the ground sloped and undulated gradually up to a long ridge, sparsely lined with trees.

"I hear 'em," Malone answered, cocking his head over to one side, listening intently.

"Do you think it's the wagon train?" William asked. "It could be, you know."

"No . . . if it is, it dang-well shouldn't be," Malone mused out loud. "That's the wrong direction all t'gether. Hell, boy, you stuck the markers in the trail, and that was way back, over there." He leaned back in the saddle and straight-legged, pulled up to study for a while. As the shooting carried on, he came to a decision. "Better go take a quick look-see. It surely sounds like trouble for somebody, don't it?"

"Think it's the snakes . . . those Indians you were telling me about?" the boy asked, his excitement showing as he spurred his horse then followed his rapidly disappearing stepfather. "If it is the Indians, what can we do? We only have the one gun."

"Ya mean . . . " — Matt grinned and pointed to himself — "I . . . only have one gun, son. And I'll do what's needed. All you've got to do, young fella, is keep yer head down an' do like I tell ya."

By the time they had breasted the next rise, the firing was reduced to only the odd, spasmodic shot. And there, in the near distance, they could make out Indian braves wearing little more than thin loincloths and thick warpaint.

Matt Malone reined in to a patch of mixed scrub and trees, dismounted and handed his horse over to the care of the boy.

"Stay with the horses, Willy. And

don't get any fancy ideas about followin' me or takin' a quick look-see." Sliding the elephant gun from its saddle holster, he fumbled as he checked the load.

"Er, excuse me sir, but how long will I have to wait?" his stepson asked anxiously. And then, blushing to the roots of his hair, went on to say, "And what do I do, if . . . ?"

Matt smiled at the boy's reluctance to finish off the question.

"Well, son, if I ain't back by dark . . . don't you waste any time comin' a-lookin' for me." Shifting the position of the hand axe so that it lay more comfortably in his belt, he dropped to his hands and knees and looked back over his shoulder.

"No! I can't do that." As game as they come, the boy stood holding the horses, chewing his lip and staring moist-eyed at Malone.

Malone shook his head.

"You can. You've got to. Just take both horses an' backtrack, like I showed ya. You can't go wrong if ya use the markers you set, then get back an' tell the major what's happened. He'll know what t' do." And just as he was about to wriggle out of cover, on his belly, he winked. "And remember, Willy, I'm dependin' on ya t' make sure ya look after yer momma, real good." Giving a last reassuring smile he said, "See ya . . . son."

There was a rustle of leaves and, as the brush closed behind him, all went silent. Except for the snuffling of the horses as they stood with ears cocked in the direction of another shot, the boy felt all alone in the world.

Occasional shots still split the air, and from time to time Matt ducked low as unpredictable ricochets whined away overhead, to die, moaning in the distance.

Crawling through a mixture of waxy-stemmed reeds and tufts of buffalo grass, he became aware of a smell:

193

a strong, human smell and, simultaneously, of the gentle splashing of water.

Malone, careful not to make a sound, put down the elephant gun and, reaching his left hand behind his back, withdrew the hand axe from his trouser belt. Absent-mindedly he scraped the ball of his thumb on the edge of the blade, unnecessarily testing its keenness. Then, with care, he transferred the haft of the tool to his still painful right hand to grip.

Raising his head a mere fraction of an inch at a time, he gazed through the thin pointed tops of the reeds until he finally spotted movement. A Shoshoni buck, perhaps seven, maybe eight feet away, stood with his feet astride, pissing carelessly against the trunk of a beech sapling.

Matt's features stayed rigid as he slowly drew back his right arm, and his eyes never blinked as he took deliberate aim.

He threw with all the strength he

could muster. The Indian's head jerked up, his arms starred and he carried on urinating as he fell slowly back. Landing with a gruff grunt on to the axe which had split the top of his spine, he quietly jerked and trembled his limbs for a short time, then lay motionless and exceedingly dead.

Still cautious, Malone took up his gun before he slithered forward and retrieved his axe. Wiping the sticky, bloodstained blade on the grass beside the inert buck, he made a mental note.

One, he told himself grimly, flexing the fingers of his wounded hand to ease them. Now, how many more are there?

With his gun gripped firmly in one hand and the axe in the other, he ignored the pain and pushed on past the ash sapling. Not until he was safely lying belly-down, behind a slight ripple in the ground, did he stop to rest and catch his breath.

On the other, steeper side of the ripple, maybe a yard or less away, he heard an Indian speak. Then two sunbrowned hands, holding a twenty pound hunk of granite, came into view. The back of the Shoshoni's head followed, then the top of his bear-greased and painted back as he stood and prepared to hurl the rock.

Malone suddenly leaned forward and, with the barrel of his gun, gave the redskin a hard push in the centre of his spine.

With a strangled cry, the Shoshoni, still holding his rock, stepped dramatically off the edge of the canyon and hurtled to his death.

Astonished by his fellow's brave suicidal leap, the other brave stood up, curious to take a quick look down the side of the cliff to see how his friend had fared.

Malone, always ready to grasp an opportunity, repeated his new party trick. A second later another surprised scream announced that the curious buck had followed his companion into space.

Gingerly, Matt scanned the edge of the canyon first to his left and then to his right. As far as he could make out, he was now totally alone on his side.

Checking across to the far side, he made out eight more Shoshoni hurling rocks over the edge.

Counting the huge brass-cased bullets in his belt, plus the ones already loaded in his gun, Matt knew that if he was careful, and correctly placed every shot where it should go, he would have two cartridges remaining.

The ground ripple where he lay helped him a lot. Without much inconvenience to his right hand, he found that he could rest the weapon directly on a thick grass tuft, and still be shielded from the enemy by the reeds in front.

Snapping the backsight up into position, he turned the knurled knob a few clicks to set the estimated range. Using his left-hand thumb, he snapped back the serpentine hammers. Then, without hurry, he cuddled the smoothly polished walnut butt against his cheek, firmly pulling the brass heelplate into his right shoulder as he settled his eye on a target.

On the opposite side of the gaping maw of the box canyon, a brave peered carefully over the edge searching for a victim. He hefted a rock high above his head.

Malone settled the foresight on the wampum medicine bag dangling in the centre of the man's chest. Then painfully he squeezed the trigger. The force required to do this was more than his healing fingers were yet used to. That slightest of delays had caused a slight shift in aim as the target moved.

The shot, when it fired, took the Indian square in the joint between the upper arm and his left shoulder. The lead bullet crumpled and plated as it struck bone, then the unfortunate buck's whole arm tore away, spinning, and spattering blood. The rock he had been holding smashed down on to his shaven skull as he folded to the ground.

"Jesus, I'm slippin' a mite. Gotta do better than that," Malone cautioned himself as he settled on where to point the left barrel. "Now, me lad . . . more application and fewer excuses."

The only buck with arrows left in his quiver began to shoot them across at him. The first flew wide by more than a yard, but the second shaft actually deflected off the right-hand gun barrel and stuck in the earth, only a foot in front of Malone's face. Unruffled, he merely resumed his original point of aim and fired.

Even as the polished bone nock of the third arrow was pressed on to the bowstring of human hair, the elephant gun spoke. As its thunder echoed, the spirit of the bow's owner was already winging its way to the lodge of his ancestors.

Matt fired two more barrels, but the wagon train attackers now kept themselves well concealed, and he missed on both occasions. But the effects of his shooting had already disheartened them. As he reloaded, they grabbed the opportunity to make a hurried evacuation.

After a few minutes of inaction from the top of the canyon, Matt heard the major shouting out from below.

"You up there, Malone?"

"Yeah . . . I hear ya, Major."

"Do me a favour?" the wagon master began. "There's some varmints in the bushes, at the tail end of the train. They've got us bottled up in here. Clear 'em out for me, will you?"

"Will do," was all Matt said. Carefully he worked his way along the canyon top to where he could position himself for maximum effect.

One Indian died. Then another two from a quick left and right barrels. There was a flurry of movement among the greenery below and he caught glimpses of Shoshoni warriors hightailing it like scalded bobtails, away from the train. He snapped off another shot and wished he had not, for he heard a scream but saw no body.

"Looks like they've gone, Major," he called out at last. Then, relieved because it was over, he rested the heavy gun on his shoulder and plodded along the edge, back to where he had left the boy. "Better be quick an' get the train out of there, Major," he yelled down. "Ya never know, that war party might come back for a second crack of the whip."

★ ★ ★

"It's all right, Willy-boy, it's only me comin' in," he called out as he approached the spot where he had left him. "The redskins are gone."

There was no answer.

Parting the branches he shoved through the bushes then stopped dead, looking around. But Willy wasn't there. Neither were the horses.

"G'damn ya boy," he growled, wanting to get back to the wagon.

At first he thought he might have made a mistake and had come to the wrong place, but the evidence was all there. The recently deposited horse droppings. Spare wands, left over from the trail marking, had been used as spears and stuck in a circular target scratched in the earth for some boyish game. Then there were the lad's clear and sturdy footprints all round the clearing.

There was no indication of any struggle and definitely no blood anywhere. But it was the faint marks of moccasins and the freshly discarded, hand-rolled cigarette butt that decided it all for Matt. The boy had been taken prisoner. Of that he was certain.

But who by . . . and why?

Malone had no answer.

11

"MY wife's what?" Malone shouted, already worried about her missing boy. Perplexed and footsore, aching and tired, and with his hand paining like it was on fire, the last thing he wanted was any further hassle. He had only just walked in to rejoin the wagon train as it was reassembling outside the box canyon, already counting the cost of the fight with the Shoshoni.

"Gone . . . missin'!"

"Missin'? How? When?" Matt raged, his left fist clenched and waved in a helpless threat to persons unknown. "Why didn't somebody stop her, for God's sake?"

"It ain't anybody's fault, Matt," the major insisted. "Nobody stopped her . . . because nobody knew she was gone, until she had."

"Oh I know it's not your fault, and I'm not blamin' you. In fact, if the truth was known, it's myself I'm blamin'. Guess that's why I'm shootin' my mouth off." He coughed a couple of times, took a hold of himself and became practical once more. "Think it was the Shoshoni?"

"Don't think so, Matt. I reckon your wife was gone a while before they attacked."

"When did ya find out?"

"Just after the lead wagon went in to the swamp." The major tugged at his side-whiskers. "But, by my way of thinkin' she was taken by somebody a while before then, somewhere before we reached the mouth of the box canyon proper, where there's plenty of cover at the sides." Releasing his whiskers he looked directly at Malone. "But that's not what a normal redskin would do. So, why just her? That's what I'd like t' find out."

The major jerked as a sudden thought struck him.

"Where's the boy . . . and come to think on it, why've you walked in without your horse?"

"Willy's gone too, Major," Malone sighed. "And so have the horses."

"Indians?"

Matt shook his head then took a drink from an iron ladle hanging on a water butt.

"Not unless we've got redskins around here who roll baccy into cigarettes." Replacing the ladle he wiped at his mouth with his sleeve. "I'm gonna need another horse to go after my wife an' kid."

"Take one of mine, the chestnut," came the immediate response. "He's dewdrop fresh, and he'll carry your weight to hell and back before breakfast." Drawing closer and dropping his voice down to a whisper, the major explained further. "I'd come with you, you know that Matt, but I've my responsibilities to the rest of the folks here. Especially now, with Indians still around, the train to get under way, and folks

205

needin' to be buried."

"Yeah, I know all that, Major. Don't worry about it. Besides, I prefer to be on my own at a time like this. I've got the stink of a rat in my nose," Malone snarled. "And it's a white rat . . . not an Indian one."

Within ten minutes, Malone, chewing the last of a quick snack, had mounted the chestnut. The elephant gun was lodged safely in an ex-army, saddle holster, and his bedroll strapped securely on to the back of his saddle.

"Don't suppose you've any idea how long this is goin' t' take, have you?"

"There ain't no way of knowin' somethin' like that," Matt shrugged. "Who knows?" Malone backed out from between the wagons, then turned the high-stepping chestnut. "I'm goin' out there t' find whoever's done this to my kin. I'm gonna get even. Then I'll fetch my missus and our boy with me . . . and I ain't comin' back here, 'til I do."

★ ★ ★

Backtracking down one side of the box canyon took valuable time and produced nothing worth while. But scouting across on the opposite side quickly yielded results.

Among the Indian sign, Mary's neat footprints formed earlier in a moist patch of earth, showed she must have been taken by surprise and snatched as she walked by the side of the wagon.

These, coupled closely to the much deeper, heavier impressions of a big-footed man, wearing high-heeled riding boots, practically told Matt most of the story.

"So," he murmured under his breath, "I was right . . . there is a white man involved. And with quality boots like that, it don't look like any woman-hungry miner t' me, neither."

Perked up now, with something positive to go on, he walked, head down, leading his horse through the bushes. He followed the clearly defined trail to the spot where his wife and the stranger had taken to the saddle and ridden away, heading south.

Within an hour's riding, Malone spotted a wisp of blue smoke drifting above a stand of pines in a narrow valley. Drawing closer, he realized the smoke was not from a casual camp-fire. Nor was it from an Indian camp-site, but curling up from the stovepipe chimney of a rough sod and log cabin, with a veranda and windows in the front.

Staying well back, and out of sight, he stopped behind a wooded hillock and tied the reins of the chestnut to a broken branch of a tree. Taking his time, he withdrew the gun from the saddle holster and checked it before making his way on foot to the edge of the wood.

From there he could look down on the cabin and, to his intense satisfaction, spotted his horse, along with the boy's and a pinto, drinking at a wooden trough. The pinto pony had dyed feathers dangling from the side of its headband, Indian style. All three were unsaddled and roaming free inside a large pole corral, at the far side of the building.

Malone was already pretty sure that the pinto belonged to the cigarette-rolling wearer of moccasins, the one who had captured his stepson and stolen the horses.

Keeping low, Matt eased himself closer, taking care not to do anything which would spook the horses and draw attention to himself. Having made it to the end wall of the cabin, he paused to listen.

Suddenly he stiffened. A voice cried from inside the building.

"No! Get off me . . . get off!" It was an English voice, filled with pain and torment.

Malone gritted his teeth. Then, with his back close to the rough log walls, he edged around the corner and along to the nearest window. After removing his hat, he peeped in through the grimy glass pane.

Matt could see it was a one-room cabin, with a table, a couple of stools and a rickety wooden bed.

On the table, his stepson was tied spread-eagled, face down, and as naked as a fried egg. No one sat on the stools, but on the bed, Mary Malone was bound and gagged, fighting desperately to free herself.

Meanwhile, standing at the end of the table, a wicked grin on his face was the breed, Little Bear.

Ducking below the level of the window, Matt made for a rusted felling axe, stuck in a well-used chopping block, halfway between the window and the door.

The boy began to yell louder, his sobs tearing at Matt. Malone set his jaw, grasped the felling axe in both hands, and kicked the door open, swinging the axe as he burst in.

Little Bear hardly had time to look up and realize he was being attacked.

The blade of the axe sliced deeply, down between the shoulder and the base of the neck, cleaving flesh and bone alike. A fountain of blood spurted over the table, drenching the boy.

Malone heaved. The axe jerked clear of the horrendous wound, and the breed, with his eyes fixed in wonder upon Malone, slumped to the dirt floor and lay still.

With scant regard for the table, Matt chopped through the rawhide straps which secured Willy.

"Get yer pants back on, boy. And stop that whimperin', you're too damned big for that . . . besides, ya ain't hurt none."

Then he turned to the bed where his wife, quiet now, lay back and wept with relief behind her gag. This time he discarded the axe in favour of his knife.

"Oh, Matt," she sobbed, as soon as she was free. Her shoulders heaved and she threw herself against him. "It's been so . . . awful!" Her arms encircled his neck and she clung on like a hungry leech. Not quite sure what to say, Matt consoled her by patting her back with his good hand and, for a moment, burying his face in her hair.

Suddenly, Mary pushed him away and her eyes looked fearfully through the open door.

"What's the problem?" he demanded before she had chance to speak.

Already she had began to scramble off the creaking bed.

"We'll have to hurry. They'll be back soon," she explained.

"They? Who the hell are 'they' . . . eh?"

"The Smiths. The mayor and his two brothers."

"Them!" He thought for a second. "Yeah, it all makes sense now. Remember that guy they hung, on the day I walked in on the wagon train?"

"Yes, why of course," she gasped, her hand flat on her mouth. "He was a Smith. Hank, if I recall correctly."

"Uh-huh, and I'll lay odds they were the same gang of bushwhackers I scared off that time shortly after."

"Where's your gun?" Willy blurted out, staring through the open doorway. "They're coming. All three of them."

Automatically, in a flash of movement, Malone's hand reached for his gun, but there was no gun . . . and no gunbelt either. All he did, was hurt his hand again. Then he remembered.

"The gun? Oh yeah, it's outside. Left it leanin' against the choppin' block," he called back, striding for the doorway.

Looking out, up the slope, he saw two riders, and a third man driving a buggy. They were a good hundred yards away, but coming directly for the cabin.

"Mary, you and the boy stay inside. Keep your heads down because there's gonna be some lead flyin'."

"But . . ." she began to object, wanting to play her part. Her word was never noticed, for he had already ducked quickly out through the doorway.

Staying below the veranda rail, Matt hefted the elephant gun and knelt behind the left roof-support of the veranda. The trio continued towards the cabin, apparently oblivious to his presence.

Fifty yards . . . forty . . . thirty . . . and the buggy pulled up hard, the driver's hand held high as a signal for the others to stop. They did.

"There's somebody there . . . behind that post, and it ain't Little Bear, neither," Adam announced from the seat of the buggy.

"It's that friggin' Malone," Abe exploded, drawing his gun and firing in the same fluid movement.

Abe's bullet struck the post with a thwack and buried itself deep in the wood, only a couple of inches from Matt's face.

With both eyes wide open, Malone swung his gun and fired without bothering to use the sights. Abe appeared to be lifted from his saddle. He fell back as the shot took him full in the centre of his chest. With both feet still trapped in his stirrups, he then hung upside down over the back-end of his mount.

Spooked by the gunfire, the animal reared up before galloping away from the scene. Its rider, bouncing head down, was being battered to a pulp by the iron-shod hooves.

"Bastard!" Adam yelled, sending another couple of bullets Malone's way. The first slug dug itself into the post exactly as Abe's had done. The second flew hopelessly high into the thick sods on the roof. The elephant gun had blasted again.

Knocked sideways, Adam toppled from the driving seat and landed on his head. He stayed that way, with one leg hanging straight and the other crooked around the nearside shaft of the buggy.

Jude's bullet was better aimed and fired from a wider angle where he could see more of Malone's body.

Matt suffered deep disappointment as well as pain when the .45 slug took him high in the right shoulder. The impact threw him backwards. He felt sick. His arm fell loosely to his side and his weapon to the ground. He spun halfway round and crashed against the log wall behind him.

"You're finished, Malone." Jude Smith cocked his leg over his horse and slid easily to the ground. The revolver never wavered a hair's-breadth, but kept pointing at Matt.

Out of the corner of his eye, Malone became aware of someone walking slowly past him, then bending down. He heard Jude laughing and taunting.

"And what, in flamin' hell, do ya think you're gonna do with that, eh?" he sniggered, standing full square on, in front of her. "Can't you count woman? That there twelve-gauge, it's a powerful big gun, but it ain't got but two barrels . . . and they've both been used up."

The last of the Smith brothers turned his attention from her and back to Matt. He leered and stood tall, lifting his head, with ultimate satisfaction written all over him.

"I always swore I'd get you, Malone. Now I have. And I've got yer woman. I'm gonna have her in a few minutes . . . I'm gonna make her wriggle like she ain't ever wriggled before." His lips curled on one side, saliva stringing on his teeth.

Taking a couple of swaggering paces closer, he stopped again to leer at Mary.

"And then, when I've finally had my fill, I'll take her to some Shoshoni friends of mine." He laughed and smirked at Mary who had the elephant gun halfway to her shoulder. "Yes ma'am, you're gonna be real surprised at what Indians can do to a woman . . . especially a white woman like you. Experts they are. First they'll all ride ya, more times than an old, one-dollar horse in a livery stable." He broke off talking and sighed.

Mary Malone placed the butt against her shoulder. She felt with her thumb for the sliding safety-catch, found it and, instead of pushing it forward, shoved it to the right. She could hear a slight click as the right-hand hammer moved over to cover another firing pin.

"You're crazy, woman." Jude grinned. "Go ahead if ya don't believe me." Raising his free hand, he placed his finger just above his nose, indicating the dead centre of his forehead. "Go on," he goaded again. "Try it . . . just there."

Mary, her face devoid of colour, kept the gun steady and levelled. She drew back the right-hand hammer with her thumb, ignoring Jude's smile as he watched her. Again he tapped his forehead. Then she crooked her finger and squeezed the trigger.

"Come on, we've things t' do, me an' you."

There followed the quietest of

bangs — almost a pop, when compared to the normal thunderous sound of that same weapon.

The fingernail on Jude Smith's pointing finger suddenly distorted, then spurted blood as the bloodied hand slipped down. Where it had been, a neat little hole could be seen.

The .22 bullet had drilled cleanly, right through the skull, lodging in Jude's brain. His mouth sagged open, while his gun-hand swung limply at his side, and his pistol dangled from his trigger finger.

Like soft toffee on a hot day, his left knee bent under him and he slowly spiralled down, finally flopping on to his back in the dirt. Still open, his dulling eyes gazed skyward and seemed to be wearing a puzzled look.

His pants back on, but still not properly recovered from his ordeal with Little Bear, Willy burst out from the open cabin door to receive a single-handed hug from his mother as she returned to Matt's side.

"There," she said with only the merest tremble in her voice, "I told you that .22 barrel comes in very handy." Then giving Malone a gentle smile, she put down the elephant gun before carefully inspecting the bloody area where he'd been shot. "It's not bad," she announced confidently. "You'll live. But, I hope you realize . . . that good shirt of yours . . . it's ruined."

THE END

ARIZONA DRIFTERS
W. C. Tuttle

When drifting Dutton and Lonnie Steelman decide to become partners they find that they have a common enemy in the formidable Thurston brothers.

TOMBSTONE
Matt Braun

Wells Fargo paid Luke Starbuck to outgun the silver-thieving stagecoach gang at Tombstone. Before long Luke can see the only thing bearing fruit in this eldorado will be the gallows tree.

HIGH BORDER RIDERS
Lee Floren

Buckshot McKee and Tortilla Joe cut the trail of a border tough who was running Mexican beef into Texas. They stopped the smuggler in his tracks.

GUNSLINGER'S RANGE
Jackson Cole

Three escaped convicts are out for revenge. They won't rest until they put a bullet through the head of the dirty snake who locked them behind bars.

RUSTLER'S TRAIL
Lee Floren

Jim Carlin knew he would have to stand up and fight because he had staked his claim right in the middle of Big Ike Outland's best grass.

THE TRUTH ABOUT SNAKE RIDGE
Marshall Grover

The troubleshooters came to San Cristobal to help the needy. For Larry and Stretch the turmoil began with a brawl and then an ambush.

HELL RIDERS
Steve Mensing

Wade Walker's kid brother, Duane, was locked up in the Silver City jail facing a rope at dawn. Wade was a ruthless outlaw, but he was smart, and he had vowed to have his brother out of jail before morning!

DESERT OF THE DAMNED
Nelson Nye

The law was after him for the murder of a marshal — a murder he didn't commit. Breen was after him for revenge — and Breen wouldn't stop at anything . . . blackmail, a frameup . . . or murder.

DAY OF THE COMANCHEROS
Steven C. Lawrence

Their very name struck terror into men's hearts — the Comancheros, a savage army of cutthroats who swept across Texas, leaving behind a bloodstained trail of robbery and murder.

FARGO: PANAMA GOLD
John Benteen

With foreign money behind him, Buckner was going to destroy the Panama Canal before it could be completed. Fargo's job was to stop Buckner.

FARGO:
THE SHARPSHOOTERS
John Benteen

The Canfield clan, thirty strong were raising hell in Texas. Fargo was tough enough to hold his own against the whole clan.

PISTOL LAW
Paul Evan Lehman

Lance Jones came back to Mustang for just one thing — revenge! Revenge on the people who had him thrown in jail.

WOLF DOG RANGE
Lee Floren

Will Ardery would stop at nothing, unless something stopped him first — like a bullet from Pete Manly's gun.

DEVIL'S DINERO
Marshall Grover

Plagued by remorse, a rich old reprobate hired the Texas Trouble-shooters to deliver a fortune in greenbacks to each of his victims.

GUNS OF FURY
Ernest Haycox

Dane Starr, alias Dan Smith, wanted to close the door on his past and hang up his guns, but people wouldn't let him.

FIGHTING RAMROD
Charles N. Heckelmann

Most men would have cut their losses, but Frazer counted the bullets in his guns and said he'd soak the range in blood before he'd give up another inch of what was his.

LONE GUN
Eric Allen

Smoke Blackbird had been away too long. The Lequires had seized the Blackbird farm, forcing the Indians and settlers off, and no one seemed willing to fight! He had to fight alone.

THE THIRD RIDER
Barry Cord

Mel Rawlins wasn't going to let anything stand in his way. His father was murdered, his two brothers gone. Now Mel rode for vengeance.

McALLISTER ON THE COMANCHE CROSSING
Matt Chisholm

The Comanche, McAllister owes them a life — and the trail is soaked with the blood of the men who had tried to outrun them before.

QUICK-TRIGGER COUNTRY
Clem Colt

Turkey Red hooked up with Curly Bill Graham's outlaw crew. But wholesale murder was out of Turk's line, so when range war flared he bucked the whole border gang alone . . .

CAMPAIGNING
Jim Miller

Ambushed on the Santa Fe trail, Sean Callahan is saved by two Indian strangers. But there'll be more lead and arrows flying before the band join Kit Carson against the Comanches.

BRETT RANDALL, GAMBLER
E. B. Mann

Larry Day had the choice of running away from the law or of assuming a dead man's place. No matter what he decided he was bound to end up dead.

THE GUNSHARP
William R. Cox

The Eggerleys weren't very smart. They trained their sights on Will Carney and Arizona's biggest blood bath began.

THE DEPUTY OF SAN RIANO
Lawrence A. Keating and
Al. P. Nelson

When a man fell dead from his horse, Ed Grant was spotted riding away from the scene. The deputy sheriff rode out after him and came up against everything from gunfire to dynamite.

FARGO: MASSACRE RIVER
John Benteen

The ambushers up ahead had now blocked the road. Fargo's convoy was a jumble, a perfect target for the insurgents' weapons!

SUNDANCE: DEATH IN THE LAVA
John Benteen

The Modoc's captured the wagon train and its cargo of gold. But now the halfbreed they called Sundance was going after it . . .

HARSH RECKONING
Phil Ketchum

Five years of keeping himself alive in a brutal prison had made Brand tough and careless about who he gunned down . . .

SUNDANCE: SILENT ENEMY
John Benteen

A lone crazed Cheyenne was on a personal war path. They needed to pit one man against one crazed Indian. That man was Sundance.

LASSITER
Jack Slade

Lassiter wasn't the kind of man to listen to reason. Cross him once and he'll hold a grudge for years to come — if he let you live that long.

LAST STAGE TO GOMORRAH
Barry Cord

Jeff Carter, tough ex-riverboat gambler, now had himself a horse ranch that kept him free from gunfights and card games. Until Sturvesant of Wells Fargo showed up.

DONOVAN
Elmer Kelton

Donovan was supposed to be dead. Uncle Joe Vickers had fired off both barrels of a shotgun into the vicious outlaw's face as he was escaping from jail. Now Uncle Joe had been shot — in just the same way.

CODE OF THE GUN
Gordon D. Shirreffs

MacLean came riding home, with saddle tramp written all over him, but sewn in his shirt-lining was an Arizona Ranger's star.

GAMBLER'S GUN LUCK
Brett Austen

Gamblers seldom live long. Parker was a hell of a gambler. It was his life — or his death . . .

ORPHAN'S PREFERRED
Jim Miller

Sean Callahan answers the call of the Pony Express and fights Indians and outlaws to get the mail through.

DAY OF THE BUZZARD
T. V. Olsen

All Val Penmark cared about was getting the men who killed his wife.

THE MANHUNTER
Gordon D. Shirreffs

Lee Kershaw knew that every Rurale in the territory was on the lookout for him. But the offer of $5,000 in gold to find five small pieces of leather was too good to turn down.

RIFLES ON THE RANGE
Lee Floren

Doc Mike and the farmer stood there alone between Smith and Watson. There was this moment of stillness, and then the roar would start. And somebody would die . . .

HARTIGAN
Marshall Grover

Hartigan had come to Cornerstone to die. He chose the time and the place, and Main Street became a battlefield.

SUNDANCE: OVERKILL
John Benteen

When a wealthy banker's daughter was kidnapped by the Cheyenne, he offered Sundance $10,000 to rescue the girl.

15.99